Darkness Awakens
Book 1

Shirayuki's Corruption

Darkness Awakens

Book 1

Shirayuki's Corruption

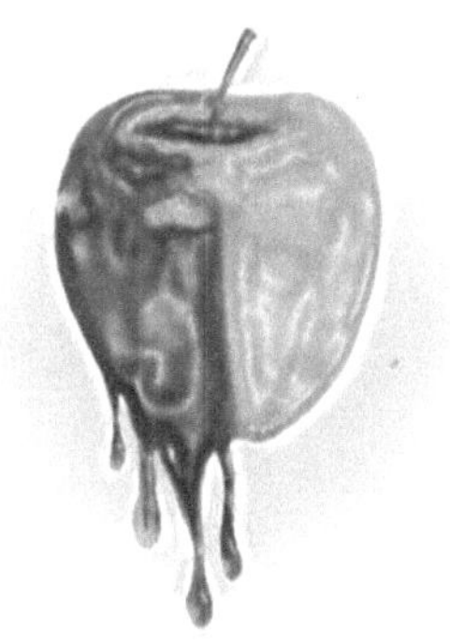

V. Kay Perks

*To Ruroni Kenshin.
The best role model a samurai girl's heart
could ask for.*

Echigo
Village
Miner's Hut
Owari
Kai
Nihon
N
NW
NE
W
E
SW
SE
S

Table of Contents

Prologue 11

Preface 19

Part 1_Yumi's Origin

Chapter 1_Mr. Fujimori 23

Chapter 2_Kagami 37

Chapter 3_My First Day 47

Chapter 4_The Mizugori 53

Chapter 5_Training 57

Chapter 6_Shopping 61

Chapter 7_100 Day Fast 67

Chapter 8_The Ceremony 73

Chapter 9_Officially an Itako 79

Part 2_Shirayuki's corruption

Chapter 10_Uesugi Kenshin 91

Chapter 11_The Proposal 101

Chapter 12_Journey to Echigo Capital 117

Chapter 13_Meeting Shirayuki 127

Chapter 14_Eavesdropping 137

Chapter 15_Necromancy 143

Chapter 16 _An Outing_ 147

Chapter 17 _Lost Princess_ 153

Chapter 18 _The Army Returns_ 159

Chapter 19 _The Argument_ 165

Chapter 20 _Shingen_ 169

Chapter 21 _Outed_ 175

Chapter 22 _The Death Poem_ 181

Chapter 23 _Broken_ 187

Chapter 24 _Vanished_ 191

Chapter 25 _Found, But Still Gone_ 197

Chapter 26 _A Mystery_ 211

Chapter 27 _Assassins on the Loose_ 215

Chapter 28 _Confirming Suspicions_ 221

Chapter 29 _Communing with the Dead_ 229

Chapter 30 _The Unthinkable Solution_ 239

Chapter 31 _A Prisoner_ 247

Chapter 32 _Kagami's Return_ 251

Chapter 33 _An Itako Forever and Always_ 259

Chapter 34 _The Funeral_ 263

Chapter 35 _Secrets Unveiled_ 269

Chapter 36_*Tokiwa* 279

Chapter 37_*Unkillable* 291

Chapter 38_*Plotting* 299

Chapter 39_*An Imaginary Note* 309

Chapter 40_*Trek up the Mountain* 315

Chapter 41_*Burned Alive* 319

Chapter 42_*Plan B* 325

Chapter 43_*A Poisoned Apple* 335

Chapter 44_*No Forever with Humans* 345

Chapter 45_*A Victorious Return* 349

Part 3_Shirayuki's Rebirth

Chapter 46_*A Wedding Invitation* 357

Chapter 47_*Revenge* 363

Chapter 48_*Death's Door* 371

Chapter 49_*Yugami* 375

Glossary 381

Character guide 387

Acknowledgements 391

About the Author 393

Book 2 Sneak Peak 397

Prologue
Uesugi Kenshin

It was just another day on the bloodied battlefield. Blood stained my clothes, and no doubt it was smeared along with dirt and grime across my face. Nothing I wasn't used to. The summer sun beat down on me and my men, causing sweat to trace tracks in the grime that has caked onto our skin.

Kagekatsu, my eldest, walked up to me as I surveyed the now silent field after the battle ended. Once filled with the shouts of men and the clang of swords ringing through the valley as men and women fought for their lives and their country. Now, it was nothing but bloodied bodies as both sides silently searched the bodies for the wounded, honoring the truce that came at dusk.

"Did you meet him?" My son asked.

"Not today." I told him.

He didn't need to specify, I knew he was talking of the Tiger of Kai[1]. I had been itching to meet the warrior in battle after hearing tales of his feats for months now.

"Is he even on the front lines?" My youngest son, Kagetora, asked.

I didn't need to look to know he was approaching from behind. He wasn't the best at hiding his footsteps yet, but that would come in time.

"He's here," I said.

My boys exchanged a look, which I noted in my peripherals.

I sighed, "Speak your minds."

"We are just worried about this new..." Kagekatsu trailed off, not wanting to offend.

"Obsession," Kagetora supplies for him.

The younger boy never worried about burning a few bridges to get to his destination.

I chuckled, reaching into my kimono[2] and

---

[1] **Kai** /kai/ - an old providence in Nihon where the Takeda clan was located
[2] **Kimono** /kee-moh-no/ A loose, wide-sleeved robe, fastened at the waist with a wide sash.

retrieving a bottle of saké[3]. Popping the cork, I took a hearty sip.

"Maybe it is an obsession," I conceded.

The boys were silent as I took another swig.

"And ..." the younger of the two asked.

"And," I sighed, putting the cork back in its place, "It doesn't change anything."

I nodded towards the horizon, pointing the bottle of saké in the direction of a lone figure.

"Is that...?" Kagekatsu asked in awe.

I put the bottle away, tucking it safely in my kimono and securing it in place with some string. I tried to school my face into nonchalance at the disappointment that stabbed my heart at the reverence my son used for this legend, but not for me, a legend in my own right.

"The Tiger of Kai," I confirm solemnly. "Help the men tend to the wounded. I have business to attend to." A smile plays on my lips at the thought of a fight that might actually pose a challenge for once.

---

[3] **Saké** /sah-keh/ Alcoholic beverage, usually a wine made from rice.

I set off down the small hill I had been standing on, making my way to the figure. Not bothering to check if my boys followed orders. I doubt they will. After all, this fight will be legendary.

***

Takeda Shingen. The Tiger of Kai. Did not disappoint. His speed and strength rivaled mine. It had been far too long since I was challenged in a fight. And I loved every single minute of it. After what felt like only moments of bliss, the duel ended in a standoff, his tessen's[4] sharp edge at my neck and my sword tip at his heart. I breathed heavily from the exertion, blowing a stray hair from my face.

Takeda's chiseled jaw ticked before he broke out into a grin, slightly lowering his tessen, but still keeping it near my throat.

"I see why they call you the Dragon of Echigo[5]," he said.

His voice was quiet and calm. I couldn't imagine him commanding an army with that voice. And yet, here we are.

"And you the Tiger of Kai," I responded.

---

[4] **Tessen** /teh-sen/ Japanese war fan. Or 'iron fan,' used as a weapon or for signaling.
[5] **Echigo** /ee-chi-go/ -an old providence in Nihon where the Uesugi clan where located.

In the light of the stars, with the full moon overhead, I could read his expression plainly. Complete bliss.

"It's been a long time," I spoke, mainly to fill the silence, "since I had anyone challenge me like you did in battle."

"Same goes for me," his eyes flicked over my shoulder, and he lowered his war fan, stepping back from my sword.

I did the same, though I didn't glance over my shoulder at what caught his eye. I wouldn't give him an opening to strike.

He collapsed his war fan, as I sheathed my sword. I extended my hand to him, and he gripped it tightly.

"It has been a pleasure crossing paths with you Takeda," I said.

"The pleasure is all mine. And please, call me Shingen."

I raised an eyebrow, "Kenshin."

"I mean, as rivals, it's only right we call each other by our first names," he squeezed my hand tighter.

I smirked as I pulled my hand out of his grip,

"care for some saké before you go?" I asked, retrieving the bottle from the folds in my kimono, popping the cork.

He eyed the bottle.

"Perhaps just a bit. It would be rude of me to refuse."

I laughed and handed him the bottle.

***

A few drinks in and we were sitting in the middle of the field, having a grand old time. When I saw a small form run from one tree to the next in the nearby forest.

I wouldn't have thought anything of it, probably just a small animal. But on a clear night like this, I saw the silhouette of a small person.

I gave Shingen a sly smile as I took another swig.

"If you're planning an ambush on me while I'm drunk it won't work, I hold my saké better than anyone I know."

He looked up, puzzled, and I gestured to the tree line with the bottle before taking another swig. The cursed thing was almost empty; luckily I had another stored away.

"Oh, that must be Shirayuki. I told her older brothers to watch her back at camp, but she must have slipped away."

He waved over to the tree line, beckoning the figure to come out.

Slowly at first, as if afraid that she had been caught, the figure emerged from the trees, then ran over to us. As she drew near, I realized the figure was a small child, a young girl no older than five no doubt. Her silk black hair shone in the moonlight as it trailed behind her. Once she was close enough she took a flying leap into Shingen's arms.

Tumbling onto his back from the impact, he laughed and began wrestling with the little girl. She fought back ferociously.

I was impressed at her form and strength for such a small child, granted Shingen was obviously going easy on her. I wouldn't know where to place my bet if she went up against one of my younger guards though.

Footsteps thundered towards us from the direction of my camp. I looked up to see my two boys running down the hill. I waved to them casually, and once they were close enough to see that I was fine, they slowed to a walk.

As they drew near, I could see that their eyes

were downcast; no doubt embarrassed that they thought I had been attacked by a rabid girl.

Upon their approach, Shingen and the young girl paused their sparring match and sat down next to each other on the grass, their clothes now disheveled and covered in grass stains and dirt.

A smile crept onto my lips.

"Ah, sorry about that," Shingen said, brushing some grass out of his hair, now falling out of its ponytail. "This is Shirayuki, my youngest. She takes it upon herself to further her training by attacking me whenever she sees me."

Shingen rubbed the back of his neck. I had trouble telling, but I could have sworn he blushed before looking down.

"No need to apologize, my friend," I said, resting my hand on his shoulder. "My boys here thought your little girl had attacked me I'm sure. Shingen, meet my sons Kagekatsu and Kagetora. - Boys, come, sit! No need to be so stiff. We are celebrating!" I raised my bottle of saké and drained the remainder of the drink before tossing it aside and fishing out my spare bottle.

Preface

I know you think you know this story. The story of a girl with skin as white as snow, poisoned by her Stepmother with an apple, doomed to an eternal sleep.

But have you ever stopped to consider that history is written by the victors? And just because they won, doesn't mean they were right, just, or good. So, this is my story. This is what really happened. Not some nice fairytale with a happy ending that makes you feel all warm and fuzzy on the inside. No, this is real life. My life.

And while I don't regret anything, I'm not sure happy is the right word for my ending.

Don't say I didn't warn you.

Part 1

Yumi's Origin

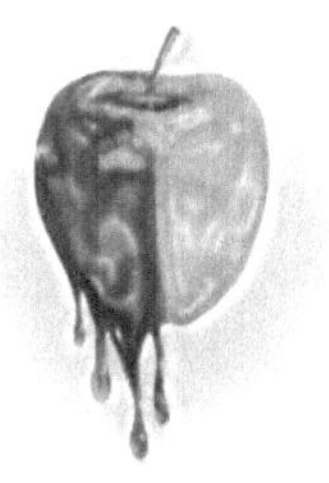

Chapter 1
Mr. Fujimori

Laughter fills my ears as I walk carefully across the uneven cobblestone path while navigating my way through the town square. My arms ache from the large parcel I am carrying. One of the corners digs into my stomach and I grit my teeth against the pain, trying instead to focus on not running into anything. I stumble on a loose stone and the laughter from across the square intensifies. I catch myself on a nearby storefront, so I don't faceplant and drop the package. I pause and take a deep breath to steady myself before I resume walking home.

I readjust the package in my arms and try my best to ignore the laughter floating closer and closer to me, instead listening intently for the sounds of footsteps in my path. But the laughter follows close behind me. Like a wounded cub it begs for my attention.

"Looks like she has gone deaf too!" I hear a young boy jest.

An explosion of laughter follows. I clamp my mouth shut and will myself to ignore it. To think of anything else. I put my full focus on moving my feet in the direction of home. I don't want to deal with these guys today. I focus my anger and hurt feelings into the speed I need to escape the town square.

Of course, all my anger does is bring up memories I was trying to block out. Memories of my mother's whispered words to my Father when she thinks I can't hear or doesn't care enough that I can.

"I knew we shouldn't have kept her," the words echo and bounce around in my head. *"She can't find work, and we know she won't be able to find a suitor. It would have been better for us if we had gotten rid of her the moment we realized she was the way that she is."*

The sharp pain in my chest swells and tears prick at my eyes at the memory. I quickly blink them away, hoping the other children didn't notice them. They would have seen tears as a victory, and I can't have them thinking there are any cracks in my armor, or else they will be even more relentless. The laughter dies down, drifting away with the wind. A few strides of quiet away from the town square tells me that they seem to have gotten bored with me and found something else to occupy their time.

I strain to hear them, just in case l am mistaken. I've become so focused on trying to listen for the children behind me, that I don't notice the soft click of footsteps coming to cross my path before it's too late.

I find myself unable to stop as the back of my hand brushes against the rough fabric of a kimono. A heartbeat later I slammed right into the legs of the owner of said kimono. I land on my backside and lose my grip on the package as I instinctively try to brace my fall. The parcel lands painfully on one of my legs before sliding off.

"Are you alright young one?" A soft, melodic voice reaches my ears.

I nod in response, and soft, gentle hands wrap around one of my wrists and begin to pull me up. At first I jerk away, realizing too late that they were trying to help me stand. But after a moment, I push off the ground with my free hand and allow them to steady me as I stand up.

A warmth spreads over me, starting at my head and reaching down to my toes, and I swear I see a flicker of bright light flash beside me. I look in that direction, but whatever the source of light was, it is gone. All I can see is the dim light of the setting sun and fuzzy blobs that should be the trees in the forest, if I am facing the direction I think I am. Either that, or it's shadows from the mountain beyond the forest.

I sigh and turn back to the person I just ran into.

"Thank you," I say bowing low to show my gratitude and respect.

"Here," the same voice says, "your package."

I reach out hesitantly. Usually when people try to hand me things, I end up dropping them. But this stranger places the package directly into my outstretched arms, not letting go until I've lifted the weight from their hands.

I smile in their direction.

"Have a nice walk," they say in a sing-song voice as the sound of their footsteps carry them away.

I listen for a moment to their footsteps scraping against the hard stone ground to make sure I know what direction they are going before I end up running into them again. Satisfied that they are heading in the opposite direction as me, I resume walking, taking care to pay better attention to what is going on around me. I have barely taken three steps, though, when the sound of their geta[6] on the hard stones stills.

I imagine the stranger turning to watch me stumble home. I listen hard for their footsteps to resume while I continue walking, holding my head high and taking careful steps on the uneven path.

Soon enough their footsteps resume. But instead of fading away, they seem to only echo and get louder. I focus on what dim light I can see ahead of me and try to decide if it's the light from the setting sun or the lanterns shining through the windows of my home.

I estimate the stranger must only be two steps behind me when I feel a hand tap my shoulder twice. I jump slightly at the unexpected contact. I reluctantly turn to face the stranger and think of how my mother will not be happy that I'll be home so late.

"Young girl, what's your name?" the stranger asks.

"Yumi." I give a bow, as is custom, and hope

---

[6] **Geta** /geh-tah/ - Traditional japanese footwear resembling flip flops with two big blocky "teeth" on the bottom.

they are not offended by my lack of addressing them with a proper title. But I find it's better to leave it off if you aren't certain who you are talking to.

"That's a fitting name, Yumi."

"Thank you," I bow again in gratitude.

This is something I hear often. My name, Yumi, means beauty. Apparently I have a natural beauty that very closely aligns with the latest trends in Nihon[7]. Long, silky, raven black hair paired with a fair complexion and red lips. Or so I'm told.

When I was younger, my mother was obsessed with me learning how to keep my hair as soft and silky as possible and how to apply my own face paints. She said that if all I had was my beauty, I needed to know how to cultivate it so I could be matched one day. That was back when she still thought my blindness might not ruin my chances of finding a suitor.

"Tell me Yumi," the stranger's voice pulls me out of my thoughts and back to the conversation at hand. "Have your parents decided what your job is to be yet?"

"No..." My answer comes out no louder and

---

[7] **Nihon** /**nee**-hon/ -Japan

clearer than a mumble, and I keep my head angled down. It's a sign of respect, but I also don't want this stranger to notice my unfocused eyes if they haven't already.

"Well, I think I have a solution that would benefit all parties. Would you be so kind as to take me to your home so I can speak with your parents?"

I nod glumly, turn back around, and finish walking home without another word. The stranger's footsteps follow behind me. Everything about this is unnerving. Never before have I had to lead someone somewhere. Usually, I'm the one being led. And then there is the *solution to benefit all parties* that I'm left wondering about. I certainly hope it doesn't have to do with marriage. I don't want to be stuck to someone for the rest of my life and have no choice in the matter. But, I suppose that I don't have much choice in the matter of what I'm going to do anyway. No one will hire someone as useless as me.

It's no longer customary to abandon blind children, though it's not completely unheard of. Some important commander or ruler made a decree that the blind were actually not a complete drain of society's resources. They were, in fact, gifted with being more in touch with the spiritual realm and should be trained in the shamanic[8] arts. My mother has tried to ship me off for training before, but people always came back with an excuse about why they weren't interested in training someone new.

My mother told me that it of course was because I was an unruly child and that I didn't even have the spiritual gift that I was supposed to, and that's why they never wanted me. This never made sense though, since I'd barely met these teachers, so how would they know if I didn't have a gift? Granted, it's not like I've seen or felt anything from the spirit realm, so I'm not saying my mother is wrong, just that we don't know for sure that I'm totally useless. At least, that's what I try to tell myself when I hear her complaining to Father that I'm a waste of food and space and that I should be contributing to the family by now.

My thoughts keep spiraling all the way home. I see the light coming through the screen in a roughly rectangular haze. I stop in front of it for a moment and take a deep breath. My fingers are numb and my arms ache from holding the parcel. I readjust it in my arms before feeling for the step with my foot and advancing onto the porch. I hear the screen slide open for me and I silently thank the stranger

---

[8] **Shaman** /**shaa**-men/ a person who acts as intermediary between the natural and supernatural worlds

with a nod of my head before ducking inside.

"Yumi!" My mother calls. I almost respond as I set the parcel down on the ground by the door, but she continues yelling. "Yumi, that better be you. You are in so much trouble; didn't I tell you that I needed these things as soon as possible and here you are coming back home at all hours of the night. What were you doi-" her words are cut short, and I assume she has now entered the room and seen our visitor. "Ah Yumi, why didn't you tell me we have a guest? I'm so sorry, I must apologize for my daughter's ill manners. She can be so oblivious."

I duck my head lower, so my mother doesn't see any emotion from my face. Calling me 'oblivious' is how she expresses her frustration in my inability to see.

"Nothing to worry about Mrs. ..."

"Watanabe," my mother supplies.

"Mrs. Watanabe, I'm the one who should apologize. I'm the reason young Yumi here is late; see, we ran into each other at the market, and I am really impressed with her. Do you and your husband have a moment to talk? I'd love to know if you're interested in me training her."

I heaved a sigh of relief that it wasn't a marriage proposal and slipped off my shoes, placing them just inside the door before feeling for the edge and sliding the screen closed.

"Oh!" My mothers voice rises a few octaves, "Oh yes. Yes! Please sit down, make yourself at home. I'll go and find my husband and make us some tea so we can talk."

I hear the soft pad of my mother's bare feet quickly retreating into the kitchen while the slower, steady footfalls of the stranger make their way to the table, where he sits on the floor beside it.

My father and mother's footsteps pad into the room. I can make out their dark shapes shrinking down onto the floor across from the stranger in the limited light flickering from the lantern in the corner. I carefully walk to the low table and take a seat as well. The smell of herbal tea wafts my way as I hear my mother filling a cup and placing it on the table. She fills two more before the stranger speaks.

"I'll cut right to the chase. My name is Fujimori. I'm a shaman, and I've been looking for an apprentice for quite some time. I've never found anyone that's impressed me as much as your daughter. I think Yumi will be very talented in the shaman arts."

My head snaps up in the direction of his voice. He sounds so sure that I would be successful. Does he really mean that? How would he know after a simple encounter of me running into him and falling on my backside?

"Are you sure Mr. Fujimori?" My mother says, and my eyebrows wrinkle. I would have thought she would jump at the chance to get rid of me, and here she is trying to talk him out of it? No wonder nobody took me as an apprentice if this is how she acted. "While it's true we have been looking for someone to take her as an apprentice, usually they start the apprenticeships around the age of 11, and she has almost reached her 14th year."

"I'm quite sure she will do perfectly. Your daughter has a gift for the arts, I can see it." Mr. Fujimori says. I hear him sip a bit of tea before his cup softly rests back on to the table.

"Well, as much as I'd hate to have my daughter move away, I can't let her pass up such an opportunity. If Yumi wishes to study with you I think this will be great for her future, and as her father, that's all I can hope for."

I smile at my father's words. "Can you tell us more about this apprenticeship?" he asks.

"Certainly," Mr. Fujimori says, "as I said, I'm a shaman and I would like to train your daughter to be an Itako[9]. It's hard work, an intensive program, and it can take up to three years for girls to complete it. But I have a feeling she could do it in a year's time. I sense she will be a natural."

Again, I wonder how he could possibly know this as he doesn't know anything about me, but I stay quiet.

"If she can complete it in that time, that would be ideal. As you may know, once a girl reaches womanhood, it can... complicate the ritual that completes the training."

"Yes I've heard that, that's why I'm surprised you would want to take on such an old apprentice," my mother says.

My eyebrows pull together. I don't think I quite understand why my age or womanhood would complicate things. I've never heard that this could be a concern, though it explains why my mother has pretty much given up on me getting an apprenticeship.

"An Itako you say?" My father reaches over and touches my shoulder, "What do you think Yumi? Would you like to train to be an Itako with Mr. Fujimori as your master?"

---

[9] **Itako** /**ee**-ta-koh/ - Blind women trained to be spiritual medians.

What do I think? Well, I think Mother will be over the moon that I will be out of the house, so she won't have to be embarrassed by me anymore. I think Father is being truthful, and that he will miss me. He will also be relieved that I would have a job and a livelihood. A way to contribute to society. But me? I don't know what I think of this particular apprenticeship, or this man who I literally just ran into on the road home. He seems nice enough and is patient with me, accommodating to my lack of sight. He also seems to think I have what it takes to become an Itako.

But is this what I actually want? Do I actually have a choice? If I said no I wouldn't hear the end of it from Mother, and apparently I'm getting too old to have another chance like this. If I don't take this, in a few short years I'd end up in the streets with no job and no husband, begging for scraps. Another opportunity won't fall in our laps like this again. This is my one chance to have a life.

"I think... this sounds... perfect," I say quietly.

A rush of warmth runs through me and sparkles of reddish light flash briefly across my vision. It's gone as soon as my panic starts to set in. I'm left blinking back black splotches that are floating in front of my already limited view of the flickering light I can see in the living room.

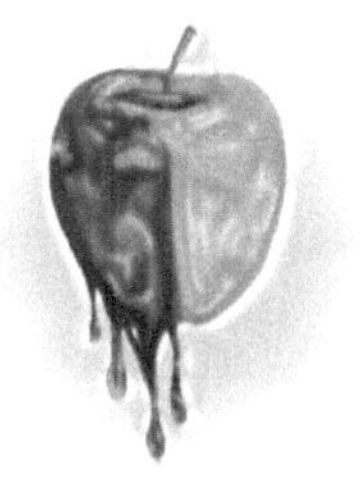

Chapter 2
Kagami

My Father packed me a small bag with some clothes and my comb, as well as soaps and the like. Mr. Fujimori said he would come at first light to pick me up when he left last night. It's been less than a day since he agreed to take me in and train me. He is eager to have me start my training as soon as possible. I try to stifle my yawn while I sit by the table with my bag in my lap. I didn't get much sleep last night; the excitement and anticipation kept me up most of the night. Nerves fluttered through my stomach, making me feel as though I'm going to vomit. I swallow, hoping to keep it down.

"Yumi," my father's heavy hand lands on my shoulder, "Mr. Fujimori is here."

I smiled up at my father, knowing it will make him happy and stand, slinging my bag over my shoulders. He pulls me into a huge hug that leaves me wanting for air by the time he releases me from his iron grip.

"You study hard, alright? You're going to become the best Itako in the whole of Nihon."

"Thanks Father," and this time my smile is genuine.

My mother bustles over and begins to fuss with my hair in the moments before Mr. Fujimori reaches our door. "You shouldn't be so careless Yumi, your looks are all you have." She complains while smoothing out my silky black hair.

I simply nodded and let her finish.

"You all set Yumi?" The melodic voice of Mr. Fujimori calls out to me from the doorway.

"Yes." I say before giving my father one last hug and falling in behind Mr. Fujimori's footsteps.

The journey to Mr. Fujimori's house is a short one, and by midday we arrive. He hardly spoke the entire way except to point out loose stones, or a slope in the road, or the occasional step. Overall, he is an excellent companion to have guide me. Mr... No. *Master* Fujimori gives me a quick tour of the small home, which includes the living room, kitchen, bath, and two bedrooms. Then he tells me he plans to step out to do some shopping.

"Go ahead and make yourself comfortable," he says before leaving. "Feel free to explore the place and familiarize yourself with the layout. But take it easy. Tomorrow your training begins, and you won't have another night off until after you are ready to be a full-fledged Itako."

"Thank you Master Fujimori." I give a bow as he slides the paper door closed with a soft scraping across the floor.

Left alone to explore, I decided to first start with my bedroom. It is plain with a simple chest in the corner for my things and a bedroll. I put my things away in the chest and as I close the lid I see a flicker of light in the corner of my eye again.

"What *is* that?" I murmur to myself, turning my head to see if the light is still there.

But it's gone. All I can see is the dim light of the afternoon sun streaming through the windows. Shaking my head, I stand, finding my way to the kitchen and living area. I walk around these rooms a few times, trying to memorize the layout. A couple of times, I see that strange flicker of light, but it's gone an instant later. Finally, I go back to my room and lay on the bedroll face down. I'm tired from the long walk over here and my mind must be so spent on memorizing this house that it's playing tricks on me.

The light is back. Even though my face is covered, buried in the blankets, I can see it right in front of me. And it's getting brighter. And... wait, is that laughter I hear? Someone must be playing a trick on me. I sit up, turn towards the sound, and jump back in surprise as a scream escapes from my lips.

***

In the middle of the bright light sits an animal. I scramble away from it until my back hits the wall, but despite trying to distance myself, despite the creature not moving, it still seems to be the same distance from me. The animal tilts its red head at me and sweeps its tails across the invisible floor it's sitting on, then lets its tails settle around itself. I blink and rub my eyes but the vision before me stays the same. The animal is a fox I decided, now that I've had time to take in all its features and compare it to descriptions of animals I've heard of in the past.

It's a stunning creature; a dark red coat I assume- it's a deeper color than what lights the sky at sunset. The bottom half of its face and chest and the tips of its seven tails are a pale color, similar to how I've heard white snow described. And its feet and ears look to be dipped in darkness itself.

"Relax, it's just me," the fox says, flicking a few tails as if to say this was obvious.

"I-I-wha- um..." I stammer over my words, unable to even think past my complete shock that I am seeing this beautiful creature in such detail in front of me.

"I'm sorry, where are my manners. I'm Kagami. Master Fujmori didn't mention me, but he should have. I'm the only reason he is training you. I'm going to be your partner. "

"My... what?"

I'll admit, I don't know a lot about the Itako profession, but I do know a few things. It is typically reserved for blind women who are trained from a very young age to commune with the dead and perform many spiritual duties during shamanic rituals. I have never heard of an Itako with a partner, much less an animal one.

"Partner," she repeats. "I told him you would be a perfect next partner, so he agreed to train you to be his successor."

"Um, okay... but... why? How can I...?"

"Oh right, I forgot. I'm a kitsune[10], so of course you can see me as I'm projecting my image directly into your mind."

Kitsune. A spirit fox said to live hundreds of years with powers of manipulation and illusions, just to name a few. My mind rattles off these facts at me as I try to process what she is saying.

"Okay... " is all I manage to say.

I must be dreaming, I think to myself.

"Of course you're not dreaming, and I can hear you, you know!" Kagami says, her ears drooping.

I squeeze my eyes shut and try to shake her out of my head, but her image remains firmly rooted in front of me, regardless of which way I look or that my eyes are closed.

"Yeah, that is not going to work. I'm projecting into your mind. No amount of... whatever that is, is going to help."

Finally giving up, I relax my face and push the loose hair away from it. "Well, can you, not?"

A hurt expression crosses her face. "Hmmm... but if I didn't then you wouldn't be able to see me."

---

[10] **Kitsune** /kit-soo-neh/ Term used in Japanese folklore that refers to foxes with supernatural abilities.

"Yeah, I'm used to that bit. What I'm not used to is a bright distracting fox floating in my vision wherever I look. It's... disorienting."

Kagami thinks about that for a bit. "I never thought of that, I suppose... Usually I simply appear as a woman or fox and walk along beside Master Fujimori, and he always enjoyed my company. I just thought, well I thought you wouldn't hate me is all."

"I didn't say I hated you! I'm not saying you need to leave. Only can you not project directly into my mind?"

Kagami pouts, letting her ears deflate before her image melts into the darkness I'm used to. I blink and my vision stays the same.

"Kagami?" I call out, my hand raises slightly as if I could touch the spirit fox.

Immediately I feel soft fur under my palm and then a weight against the side of my leg.

"I'm still here Yumi," Kagami says, "and you don't need to speak aloud. I can hear your thoughts just as clearly as your words."

Okay... I think.

"You know, Yumi, you're entirely too trusting?"

"What do you mean?" I ask aloud.

"A powerful spirit appears to you, a kitsune no less. You do know the kind of powers a kitsune have, right?"

"Yeah...."

"And here you are trusting every word of what I have to say. You're lucky I don't mean you any harm or else you'd be done for."

My hand stills in her fur.

"Oh, no need to be upset, it's good that you're trusting. It's a quality I admire in my own unique way,"

Her words do little to settle the unease that has now risen inside me, and I make a mental note to verify her story with Master Fujimori when he gets back.

"That's good," Kagami says, "trust but verify. Yes, I think I made a fine choice for my next partner."

Partner? I think again remembering my earlier confusion.

"Well, of course, I can't be Master Fujimori's partner much longer. He is quite old, and he refuses to let me use any more magic on him to extend his life. He wants to simply get old and die. So lame. But he told me before he does I get to choose who he trains to be my next partner. You!"

"Were you there then, when I ran into him at the market?"

"Of course! If you had sight you would have seen me as a beautiful young woman on his arm, but being a spirit, you wouldn't have heard my footsteps, though. I didn't get a very good peek at your mind. You noticed my presence right away, so I withdrew. Didn't want to freak you out..."

"Wait. The light, that warm feeling. That was... that's you?"

"Yes. Master Fujmori wasn't lying when he said you had a gift for the spiritual arts. You are very sensitive to our touch."

Chapter 3
My First Day

The next morning, I woke with a soft pelt of fur bundled beneath my arm. It shifted and let out a dramatic sigh, startling me as I realized it was a living being. I just about flew off my cot and flung myself across the room before I remembered that it was probably just Kagami. I rested my hand against my thundering chest and tried to calm my racing heart. Under my free hand, Kagami placed her head gently into it and nuzzled me with her soft fur.

"Good morning," she yawned and withdrew for a moment, and I imagined she was stretching.

"If you're a spirit," I asked, "how can I feel you, but I can't hear your footsteps?"

"My physical form isn't simply an illusion that I use when I wish to appear visible to humans. It would be completely impractical if I couldn't interact with this realm. I can appear as more than just an illusion if I want to, and usually I do. What you feel is my physical form, but I'm practically weightless with being a spirit and all, so I hardly make a sound when I move. I'm sure if there were zero other noises around and you strained your ears very hard you could hear me move about."

"oh, okay, well thanks for not projecting into my consciousness," I said. "It really messes with my spatial awareness. I like interacting with you like this, you have very soft fur."

"Why thank you Yumi. You know, I think we will get along just fine if you can make compliments like that."

I laughed. A good proper laugh. As I swiped a stray tear from my eye I realized I didn't know when the last time was that I laughed like that.

"As fun as chatting with you is, the sooner you finish your training the sooner the real adventure begins. So, if you don't want the first day of your training to be any worse than it already will be, I'd suggest eating some breakfast while you still have a chance." Kagami said this so casually as she walked past me, letting my hand trail along her back as if she didn't just drop a huge mess of questions in my lap.

"What do you mean worse? What is going to hap-"

"Nuh uh, I'm not wasting anymore time explaining things to you! Just know that you, being a frail human, will need your energy, so you should go eat some breakfast."

I dragged my fingers through the tangles in my hair, figuring that would be good enough for now. I knew my mother would not approve, but I didn't have to worry about her fussing about my looks today. I hurried to the door; I'd slept in my kimono from yesterday so I didn't bother changing. As I reached for the door handle I asked, "so you're really not going to-"

"No more questions! Only eating!"

Kagami butted her head against my legs, urging me towards the kitchen. I grumbled about being bullied by a spirit fox who wouldn't even let me finish a simple question as I walked into the kitchen.

"Ah good, you're awake, you almost missed breakfast," the soft singsong voice of Master Fujimori greeted my ears upon entering the kitchen.

"Told you," Kagami gloated, but I ignored her.

I heard Master Fujmori slide a dish across the low table in my direction and I sat down by it. Finding some chopsticks resting on top of the bowl, I started eating. The rice was cold.

"And I see you have met Kagami, I trust you are getting along well."

I nodded, "She gave me quite the shock."

"She loves me," Kagami insisted.

Master Fujmori laughed, "Well good, considering I'm only training you for Kagami's sake. I'm glad you two seem to be getting on okay."

"Why are you training me anyways?" I rushed on to explain, "I mean, why for Kagami, I didn't think kitsune liked people very much."

"True, it's rare for a kitsune to bond with a human, but not unheard of. Kagami took pity on me and saved me from drowning when I was just a little boy. I think she was more motivated by her dislike of the water spirit who had me in her grasp than any actual sympathy. Don't give me that look, Kagami, I know it's true! But it doesn't change the fact that she became attached to me not long after that. She is a wild card- always has a trick up her sleeve. I never put up with her nonsense, though. I think perhaps she likes the challenge. Anyway, I'm getting on in years and I'm ready to retire. She is quite upset with me about it. So to make it up to her I promised I'd train her a new partner."

"Don't you have friends, other kitsune in the spirit realm that you would want to go back to?" I asked Kagami.

"Ugh! It's so boring there. It's always this and that and nagging and bragging about how many human spirits they have driven mad or eaten their souls. It gets boring after a while. Here though, there is always so much drama about everything. Even if none of it matters, you silly humans make it matter! Now *that's* entertainment."

"But, I don't understand, if all you want is a companion, why don't you just go make a friend? Why do I need to be trained as an Itako?" I realized as I was speaking that I should shut my mouth before I talked myself out of a job. Oh, my mother would love to hold that over my head. *'Yumi's so useless she convinced her master that he didn't need anyone to train after all in less than a day on the job.'*

"Well, you don't need to, but it's easier for her to bond with someone with a gift for the spiritual arts. She can be honest about her nature and you're more likely to be open to friendship. And I figure she is very helpful when it comes to that sort of thing, so, might as well train you to strengthen your gifts."

I nodded and shoveled the remainder of my rice into my mouth, not trusting myself to ask another stupid question.

"Once you become an Itako, we will be an unstoppable team." Kagami insisted.

"Now Kagami, no corrupting my student. She isn't here to learn how to play tricks and mess with people, she is here to learn how to be a powerful shaman. That being said, the first thing we need to do is a mizugori[11], then you will begin your recitations."

My throat plummeted to my stomach forming a hard rock. I tried to swallow, "Yes, Master Fujimori."

---

[11] **Mizugori** /mee-zoo-**goh**-ree/ cold water ablutions for the purpose of purifying the individual before or during an important event.

Chapter 4
The Mizugori

After changing into a white sheet that I wrapped tightly around myself, I stood in the brisk morning air out in front of my Master's home. Kagami kept telling me to relax, but my grip on my own arms just kept getting tighter and tighter. I had heard stories about what the training for an Itako was like, but I never actually applied those horrors to myself. And here I was standing out in the cold just waiting to be even colder still.

"It's really just a formality," Kagami was droning on about how relaxed I should be, "It shouldn't last long, Master Fujimori doesn't like that these are even a part of the Itako training. But it's necessary to do things by the book if you want to get the proper certification and be free to practice the shamanic arts throughout Nihon."

She. Just. Wouldn't. Stop. Talking.

It was one thing to let me know it would be quick; it was another to tell me it was only going to get worse from here on out. She kept saying *this* time it will be short. *This* time is no big deal. But what about the next time? And what about the end ceremony? I shuddered just thinking about what I would be put through when I completed this training.

All thoughts of the future swiftly left my mind the moment I was hit with the first bucket of ice-cold water pouring on top of my head. I gasped and stifled a scream, fighting every rational thought I had to run to the warmth of the house. Instead, I stayed put and waited for the next bucket of water to come.

Sure enough, it hit.

I sputtered as some water made it into my mouth. I lost track of how many buckets were dunked repeatedly over my head, but eventually I was left shivering in a puddle of freezing water. Every slight breeze felt like icicles stabbing into my wet skin. I couldn't feel my feet, or my hands, or my ears, or nose. I was shaking uncontrollably. I couldn't hear Master Fujimori over the chattering of my own teeth. Kagami wrapped me in her warmth and gently led me inside, speaking softly into my mind. "Master Fujimori says you did great and it's time to get warm, come along." I stumbled over my feet and for the first time in a long time, I felt completely helpless without my other senses working to help me compensate for my lack of sight.

***

Once I was dressed in dry clothes and sitting in front of the warm fire, I thought I would feel much better. But instead, I felt so much more pain as the blood began pumping new life to my frozen extremities. My teeth chattered on for a long time. When the pain finally relented, and I could speak without jittering like a squirrel, I began my lessons.

My lessons consisted of vocal exercises to help me to be able to pronounce the words to rituals correctly and project my voice so I could be heard in the spirit world. And of course, repeating the words to various rituals and trying to commit them to memory.

When we had finished it was almost nightfall, but Master Fujimori gave me a list of chores to complete before I could finally rest. Kagami helped me out a lot with the chores. Whenever Master Fujimori wasn't around, she would whisper helpful directions or help me lift the firewood.

When I was finally done, I helped make dinner for us. Then I inhaled my food before finally collapsing into my bed.

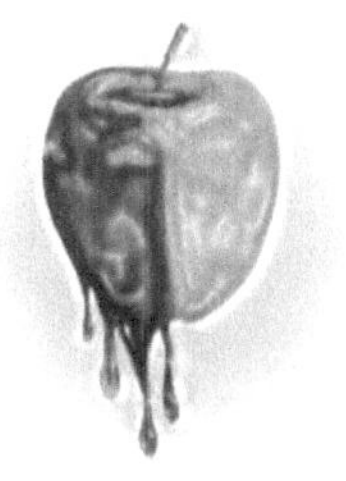

Chapter 5
Training

The next day wasn't as bad. I didn't have to endure a mizugori at least. I spent the morning making and cleaning up breakfast, then we spent most of the day doing vocal exercises and memorizing rituals. Master Fujimori was much harder on me today than yesterday. I didn't imagine that he could have possibly been going easy on me after what he put me through yesterday, but he was definitely less patient today.

"Louder Yumi! No more mumbling, you must be heard the first time, now try again!" He smacked his hand down on the table with a loud bang to emphasize his point.

My throat ached and my legs were stiff from standing in the same place all day. I repeated the line back to him louder this time.

"Now the pronunciation is all wrong. Again!" His hand hit the table once more.

I flinched and tried again.

When the lessons were finally over, I was given another list of chores to do before I was expected to make dinner.

***

That night, I lay in bed exhausted, sleep just about to take over, when Kagami pressed her head against my hand urging me to pet her before resting her head on my stomach.

"Long day?" she asked.

"Where were you all day?" I asked groggily.

"Making mischief. Fujimori says I'm not allowed to help you because it would be cheating, and while I take great offense that he doesn't want me around during your training, I also kind of agree. You have the ability to become a great Itako and relying on me too much wouldn't help you. That being said... I'll still come help you out a little when Fujimori isn't paying attention. Not enough that you're relying on me, just enough to speed the process along."

"Mmm, thanks." I said sleepily. "I feel like he is pushing kind of hard. It's only my second day, and he expects me to be perfect."

"Training can take up to three years. He is worried that both of you are too old for that to be a realistic timeline. So, he is pushing harder than he would otherwise."

"I'm too old?" I say through a yawn, relishing that I can mumble without being yelled at right now.

"Yes. Once you are a woman, the ceremony might not take at the end of your training. And since we don't know when your monthly bleeding will be upon us, we are racing against an invisible clock, especially since it really should have started already.

"Can't you stop the clock? You're supposed to be.... " I almost lost my train of thought as my eyelids slid closed, "all powerful or whatever."

"Come now, you can't believe everything you hear. Now rest."

I nodded and let my eyes slide the rest of the way closed, falling instantly into a blissful sleep.

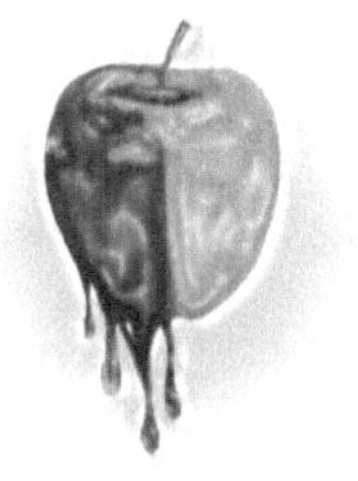

Chapter 6
Shopping

My days were spent much the same for almost a year. A few chores in the morning, lessons all day, and more chores before bed. Kagami kept me company as much as she could when Master Fujimori was feeling more trustful that she wouldn't interfere with my training. I caught on quickly with the rituals, and eventually Master Fujimori stopped yelling as much and returned to his cheerful self, though he was still very strict with my studies. Thankfully, my monthly bleeding still hadn't started yet, I wasn't sure exactly why it was such a big deal, but it had to do with interrupting the final purification ritual that lasted for 100 days.

Finally, the day came when I was able to recite every ritual needed to be an Itako perfectly every time. I was so happy when I mastered the last one that Kagami and I danced around in the middle of the lesson. Master Fujimori grunted disapprovingly but let me have the rest of the week off from chores so long as I kept reciting the rituals for him once a day.

That week was amazing.

While I had grown strong over the past year and the chores didn't bother me much now, it was nice to not have to do the laundry and collect firewood and make all the meals for once. I knew Master Fujimori was spoiling me because he felt bad about what I would have to endure next, but I tried not to dwell on those depressing thoughts and instead enjoyed my freedom.

***

The last day of my week off Kagami convinced me to go shopping with her. She manifested in her human form instead of her fox one for the day. Disguised as a young woman she linked her arm through mine as we walked into town. By this point I just accepted that somehow her illusions were a little more substantial than the word 'illusion' let on. She could interact with the world and everything in it in whatever form she pleased, and I was just grateful she wasn't floating around in my subconscious.

She steered me directly into the first clothing

store she could find and immediately began gushing over all the beautiful kimonos they had on display.

"Oh, this color would look amazing on you!" She ran the silky fabric over my fingers and in the low lantern light of the shop I could tell it was a paler color. Yellow perhaps.

"It feels amazing," I agreed.

"Too bad we are only looking for a white and red kimono for the ceremony," Kagami sighed and dropped the kimono sleeve.

Typically, the master would find a suitable outfit for their Itako to wear in the final ceremony, but Master Fujimori wasn't looking forward to going shopping for kimonos and agreed to let Kagami come and pick them out.

"Oh! This one will do for the purification rituals," She brightened up and pulled me along to her next inquisition.

I tried to tamp down the nerves churning in my stomach over the mention of the purification ritual. That was a necessary part of my becoming an Itako, but it was not something I was looking forward to.

"It's a little bland but Master Fujimori insisted that the white one look as much like a burial shroud as we could get, which is totally depressing."

I nodded in agreement. The initiation lasted 100 days, ending in the ceremony. During those 100 days I'm expected to fast and wear a white kimono similar to a burial shroud to symbolize death and then rebirth as I emerge a full-fledged Itako.

"Well, I suppose I'll have them wrap this up for you while we look for the red one," Kagami walked away to give the shopkeeper my white kimono.

I wandered through the shop, running my hands along the various kimonos. Some had intricate designs embroidered along the sleeves while others were a sturdy cotton. One caught my attention as my hand skimmed over it. I lifted the sleeve and ran my hand over the design. I could tell this one was a darker color. A deep blue or maybe even a rich red. I was fingering the tiny beads sewn into the silk embroidery when I heard Kagami gasp.

"That's perfect!"

I looked up in her direction, "did you find a red wedding gown?"

"*You* found a red wedding gown, and it's amazing!"

"This one? It has such an interesting design," I said, running my hand over the design of flowers and vines.

"And here I thought I would have a whole day of shopping with you, but we are already done," Kagami flashed an image of a sad fox puppy face in my mind for just a moment to really emphasize how disappointed she was.

I laughed and blinked the image away, "We can still check out some of the other shops before we go home if you really want to."

"Oh yes! Can we? And we are going to eat beef pot for lunch too! My treat."

"Do I want to ask how you have money to pay for this?"

"Hmmmm..... probably best not to question it."

Kagami grabbed the kimono from me and pulled me along to get it wrapped up for us while we shopped around other places.

By the time we got home, I was exhausted from being dragged along to shop after shop. Not to mention the hours-long journey there and back to the master's home. I had forgotten how busy and noisy the market could be. I hadn't ventured into town for nearly a year; most of my chores were around the house and surrounding yard. But being back was surreal. I remembered where most of the shops were. I even recognized a lot of the shopkeepers' voices, at least the ones I'd frequented before. Yet something felt different. Everyone got quiet when I walked by and whispered to each other in hushed tones. It used to be that they didn't bother to talk about me loudly, as if being blind also made me deaf. I wasn't sure if this was because they knew I had been gone for so long because I was training to be an Itako. Or if they knew my initiation was starting soon. Or perhaps it was the presence of Kagami on my arm, no doubt in the form of the most stunning young woman she could imagine.

I collapsed onto my bedroll upon returning home. I tried to appreciate the softness of the blankets knowing I wouldn't be sleeping in this bed for the next few weeks. I left the window shutters open and let the crisp cool night air drift across me as I closed my eyes and drifted off into blissful sleep.

Chapter 7
100 Day Fast

While we were away at the market yesterday, Master Fujimori spent the day making a small shed in the yard for me to spend my 100 day fast in isolation. It was stocked with what little foods I was permitted to eat along with many buckets of water. In the corner was a deep hole for me to relieve myself. The first day wasn't so bad. I passed the time counting my preserves and separating them in piles for each day I would be in isolation. This way I wouldn't eat too much and be left completely starved by the time the last week came along.

At night it was worse. The thin walls did little to keep the chill at bay, I curled up in the corner of the small room and tried my best to let my kimono swallow me up and trap in as much heat as possible.

Kagami came sometime before dawn to visit.

My teeth were chattering and all I could think about was that it would only get colder as the seasons wore into fall.

"How are you holding up?" Kagami's voice was a soft whisper directly into my mind.

Why are you whispering? I thought. *No one can hear you.*

"Yes but Master Fujimori has been watching me like a hawk telling me not to interfere. If he senses my energy too close to you, he might banish me from the property until after initiation."

Every time she spoke, a touch of warmth would begin spreading from my center, but as soon as she was done talking, all too soon the cold would seep back in. My best guess was that she only ever stayed present long enough to speak and then darted away to avoid detection. I wasn't exactly sure how powerful Master Fujimori was, he never demonstrated his powers for me, but I knew he was a necromancer[12]. Very similar to an Itako but with a different specialty in raising the dead. Necromancy is a difficult business, so I knew he had to have a strong connection and command of the spirit realm

---

[12] **Necromancer** /neh-**kroh**-man-ser/ a person who uses shamanic rituals and magic to reanimate dead people or to foretell the future by communicating with them.

and its inhabitants.

Perhaps you should listen to him. I thought.

"And leave you all alone? No, I'll still visit from time to time."

I smiled. I didn't quite understand why Kagami was so fiercely loyal to Master Fujimori, and now me, but I was very grateful to have her as a friend. Kagami was silent for a long time, so I supposed she had to leave for good. I tried to go back to sleep, but it was difficult with the cold and the growing ache in my stomach letting me know I hadn't eaten enough the day prior. Somehow though, I was able to drift off.

***

The days passed in a semi sleepless haze. I would slowly eat through the meager rations of potatoes and yams each day and pass the time repeating the rituals I had memorized over the past year. At night, Kagami usually visited when she was sure that Master Fujimori was sleeping. I did my best to sleep, but it wasn't very restful with my growing hunger and the cold hard ground making it impossible to be comfortable. Then, just before dawn every morning, Master Fujimori would come and wake me for a round of cold-water ablutions[13]. I dreaded each morning when Kagami would leave, knowing that her departure meant sunrise was approaching and soon I would have to endure an even more intense cold than even the night could provide. I would stand outside of the hut in just my slim underdress as he thrust about 10 buckets of ice-cold water on me before helping me back into the hut for more isolation. I'd slip back on my kimono to attempt to dry off and warm myself, before eating through my rations for the day.

Finally, I was down to my last small pile of rations. Either this was the last night of sleeping on the cold ground, or I had seriously miscalculated. I curled up in the fetal position trying to stay warm and relished in the thought that I was almost there. Creeping doubts and worry tried to seep their way into my mind of what trials tomorrow would bring.

However, I was already too weary and too cold to put much effort into such demoralizing thoughts. Instead, I focused on the feast they would have at the end of the day. Tons of red rice and fish to fill my belly to the brim for the first time in months! My stomach grumbled and my mouth began to salivate. *Just one more day...* I thought, as a fitful

---

[13] Ablution /ah-*bloo*-shon/ Purification method involving dumping cold water on the subject repeatedly.

sleep took over.

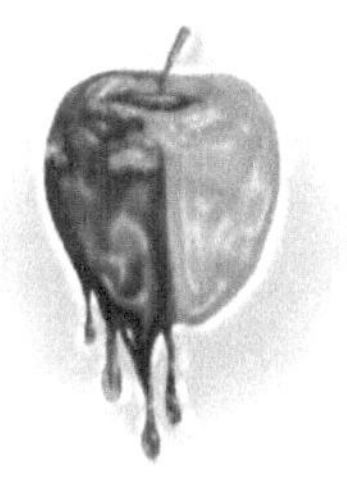

Chapter 8

The Ceremony

I woke to the sounds of people milling about outside the shed. It was the dead of the night- I could tell by the temperature of the air and the night creatures chirping in the woods not too far from where I lay on the hard ground. I sat up and rubbed my eyes to get the crusty corners free. The ceremony was beginning.

***

I heard the door creak as it opened and I rose unsteadily to my feet using the wall of the shed to help me remain upright. I knew the whole town was invited. That my parents would be there, along with many other shamans who traveled here to help with the ceremony.

"Are you ready Yumi?" It was my father's

voice.

Tears sprang into my eyes. My hand shook as I tried to raise it to my face to wipe away the tears. My father's gentle grasp steadied me as he put his arm around me. He led me onto the stage they had constructed for the ceremony. It was made of smooth wood that was cold against my bare feet. My father let go of me, stepping away, letting the brisk Fall breeze seep into my clothes. The white kimono I had been wearing the past few weeks, no doubt no longer white, was removed and I was left in just a white under slip. I felt completely alone and exposed in the cold air that dawn had yet to warm.

That's when the first bucket of water hit me. I should have expected it. I should have been used to it by now. But I seriously doubt anyone could get used to the sensation of ice-cold water being dumped on you, whether you're expecting it or not. Another bucketful of water hit me, and I struggled to keep my knees from buckling. More buckets kept coming. I spat out the water that found its way into my mouth.

By the fourth bucket I couldn't stand any longer and sank to my knees. I lost count of how many times the water assaulted me. I stopped trying to keep the thick wet strands of hair from my face. It was too much to even kneel. My hands hit the wood as another bucket of water hit me. I wanted to curl up on the ground and wait for it to be over. I thought this was a wonderful idea and began leaning toward the welcoming cold wet ground. Before I hit the deck and collapsed completely, strong arms caught me and propped me back up into a standing position.

"I got you baby girl," I thought I heard my father's voice whisper over the chatter of my teeth.

He held me up and endured the water ablutions with me until they had finished throwing one thousand buckets. I'm certain I blacked out soon after my father held me upright, because the next thing I knew I was being lifted up and carried into the warmth of Master Fujimori's home. My father laid me on my bedroll and wrapped me up in a towel.

My mother and Kagami helped me dress in a fresh white kimono, the one me and Kagami picked out just over a hundred days ago. They did up my hair and added a veil to complete the burial shroud look. Then my mother fought my still shaking hands to get white gloves on me while Kagami risked being kicked while putting on my leg coverings.

When I was dressed, they helped me back into

the main room in the house for the kamituke[14] ritual.

The low table we usually ate at had been moved into another room to allow space for the ceremony. So, there I stood, right where the table should be, surrounded by shamans from across the region. I bowed to the four points of the compass with the help of Kagami. Typically, my master would assist me in standing throughout the entirety of the ritual. But as it would last for hours, and Master Fujimori was not as strong in his old age, they permitted Kagami to take his place.

The shaman around me began to chant.

The words were foreign and swirled in and out and around my head. I wasn't really conscious at that point, but I knew I had to stand and that when this was over I'd get to eat. But first I had to do something. I didn't know how much time had passed when the chanting finally subsided. The handle of a paint brush was placed in my hand.

"Sweep it along the floor" a whisper echoed louder than the chanting still bouncing around in my head. I did as the voice instructed. I realize now it was Kagami. She was whispering instructions in

---

[14] **Kamituke** /kah-mee-too-keh/ a ritual performed during an Itako's final ceremony to determine which deity will claim them as their 'bride' and be their patron granting them power to commune with the spiritual realm.

my mind so that I wouldn't embarrass myself. As a part of becoming an Itako I needed to be recognized by one of the gods. One way to do this was to sweep a wet paint brush across the floor with strips of paper, each containing a name on the floor. The one that sticks claims you as theirs and you became their bride. Symbolically.

Remembering that this was one of the more common ways to find out which god would choose me, I gripped the brush. I almost dropped it in the haze of my barely conscious state, letting it clatter to the ground from my weak grasp. But I adjusted my grip and swept it in an arch along the ground in front of me.

The room grew silent as an old, wrinkled hand took the brush from me. A matching old and withered voice of a woman, probably a shaman, read the name that had caught onto my brush.

"Tsukuyomi, the god of the moon!" Cheers filled my ears, and I collapsed against Kagami as the world filled with darkness.

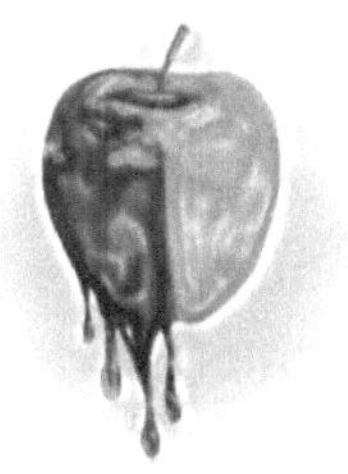

Chapter 9
Officially an Itako

I woke in my cot with the familiar feeling of soft fur under my hand. Hunger stabbed at my stomach, and I knew if I tried to sit up the world would begin spinning around me. I pried my eyes open and saw the faint light streaming in through the window, signaling that it was almost nightfall.

"You're awake!" My father's voice rang in my ears.

"I'm hungry," I said, trying to blink away tears.

"We were waiting for you before we started the celebration, I'll take you to the feast."

"Don't I ....I need my red dress, right?

"You are already in it. Your mother and your friend dressed you after you passed out so you could eat as soon as you woke up."

It took a great deal of effort to move my hand to touch my kimono and feel the intricate flower design and beads embroidered onto it.

"Oh," is all I could manage.

My father's strong arms lifted me from my bed roll and carried me outside where they had set up tables and cushions for people to sit and eat. Once we were outside, he set my feet on the ground, and I whimpered in protest.

"It's okay, the seat of honor is only about five paces away and your plate is already filled. You can make it."

I leaned heavily on his arm and shuffled forward as he guided me to my seat.

It wasn't until I had eaten most of my rice that I finally turned to him and said "You lied. It took me at least ten paces to reach the food."

He laughed. "Well, I guess I was judging a normal pace, not a starved one." I smiled at him before I shoveled more rice in my mouth.

My belly filled quickly, and I only ate a few bites of fish, opting for the more bland foods that would be easier for my stomach to handle. Still, by the end of the night I felt like I would burst the seams of my kimono.

The celebration lasted well past midnight. When the guests were finally tired out from dancing, eating, and drinking, they all left but for the few who piled in the house to sleep a few hours. These consisted of my parents and a few shamans who would be present when I was given my certification and tools.

Since this was supposed to be my wedding ceremony for my union with the god of the moon Tsukuyomi, the wedding needed to be consummated. Master Fujimori always glanced over that part as if it was unimportant. But as I waited in my room for him to act as proxy for the god, I was relieved when he never showed. Kagami appeared just before I drifted off and told me the other shamans would think he entered my room to fulfill this role, but it was just an illusion to keep them happy.

I sighed with relief. Master Fujimori wanted me to be fully certified so I could contribute to society, but even he liked to bend the rules when he could. Kagami wore off on him I suppose, though I doubt he would ever admit to it. Sleep came easily after that.

Morning, however, came all too soon with Kagami nudging me with her snout saying it was time to get up and get dressed. I combed through my hair, tied it back in a high ponytail, and put on my most comfortable kimono. It wasn't my nicest and Kagami pouted when I told her I didn't care if it wasn't nice enough; this wasn't as big of a deal as the ceremony the day prior. I just needed to be presentable, and quite frankly, I was ready to be comfortable in my own clothes now that I had the option again.

I met Master Fujimori in the living room that was adjoined to the kitchen and sat at the low table across from his usual place. He greeted me cheerfully when he saw me emerge from the kitchen.

"Yumi! I was just about to send your mother to help you get ready, I trust you slept well?"

"Yes Master Fujimori, thank you," I glanced about the low-lit room and saw many shadows blocking the natural light from streaming in through the windows. I assumed they were the other shamans from the region and my parents. Maybe a few other guests who stayed the night to see me be presented with my certification.

"Well now, let's get this over with so we can get some breakfast, yeah?" Master Fujimori said, and a few people coughed behind him.

"Yumi, this is your certification. This proves that you went through the required trials and successfully completed your training to be an Itako. It is proof that you can legally practice the shamanic arts throughout Nihon."

He handed me a small stack of papers and I ran my hand over them reverently. I couldn't read them, obviously, but I could tell they were filled with ink, most likely detailing my qualifications.

"And this," he placed a length of bamboo in my hand, "is where you can keep them."

I examined the bamboo in the low-lit room. It was dark, covered in some sort of lacquer to preserve it which I think also colored it black. I set down the papers and felt for the ends of the bamboo. There was a cork in either end so I could roll up the papers and keep them in there without them falling out. Attached to each end was a strip of leather, creating a single strap so I could sling it over my shoulders and wear it across my back.

I uncorked one end, resulting in a resounding pop that echoed through the quiet room and rolled up my papers as tight as I could before slipping them into the tube and re-corking it. Then I slung the strap over my head and adjusted it until the tube rested comfortably on my back.

When I was done, I heard the scrape of wood against wood as Master Fujimori slid an object towards me.

"And this is everything you will need to fulfill your role as an Itako."

I reached out and felt a small wooden box. Finding a small clasp, I undid it and gently lifted the lid. As I explored the contents of the box, I heard the other shaman in the room shift in their seats. Whether they were impatient or wanting to see, I didn't know.

I ran my fingers over a length of beads and some bones strung together. There were also small bundles that I guessed had some rice and salt so I could perform rituals whenever I was called upon, as long as I was fully stocked. It also contained other wooden figures and trinkets that I would need for some rituals.

I decided I could examine them later in private. For now, I slipped the necklace of beads and bone over my head and gently closed the lid and did the latch, running my hands reverently along the top and down the side of the box. My fingertips caught once more on a length of leather so I could secure it to my person.

I turned my attention towards Master Fujimori

again.

"Yumi, you are officially an Itako, congratulations!"

I heard a collective sigh as if every shaman in the room was holding their breath throughout this exchange. I heard my mother stifle a sob. My father's voice whispered hoarsely, "We are so proud of you." I beamed at the room.

The shaman who traveled here took turns congratulating me and welcoming me as a member of the shamanic arts before they left on their various journeys home. Soon it was just me and my parents with Master Fujimori, eating breakfast at the table. My father was talking about how glad he was to be able to have me back at home and how proud he was of me completing my training so quickly. I told them I was excited to come home as well and assured them that my pet fox would be no trouble at all.

My mother didn't seem too keen on the idea of me bringing home a fox to live with them. And while Kagami suggested to me that she could appear as a woman, I preferred her in her fox form. Her fur was comforting, and it reminded me that she was a powerful spirit and I needed to keep an eye out for her mischief.

But eventually we decided that Kagami could come, Mother getting out-voted on keeping her outdoors. So, I went to go pack up my things for the long journey home.

My life after that was happy. I was called upon whenever someone required my services. I attended many funerals and communed with the dead often. Everything seemed simple and normal. Well, that is, until *he* showed up.

Part 2

Shirayuki's Corruption

1 year later

Chapter 10
Uesugi Kenshin

It was a Tuesday.

He knocked on the door to my family's house. My mother answered it, leaving me to finish cutting the vegetables for that night's dinner. My mother became very flustered, inviting him in and insisting he sit down. I heard his deep and commanding voice ask, "I heard that Yumi the Itako lived here. I wish to ask for her services."

"Yes! Yes. I'll go get her, please make yourself at home."

My mother bustled into the kitchen and clung to my arm, whispering fiercely. "Yumi, the Daimyō[15] Uesugi Kenshin is here to request your

---

[15] **Daimyō** /**dah**-ee-mee-oh/ feudal lords who acted as vessels of the Shogun in their province.

services. He is very handsome, and you know, I heard he hasn't married yet! I know he is rather old, don't give me that look! His guard is quite nice too. That would be a huge status boost," She chattered away furiously, fussing with my hair as I wiped my hands clean and removed my apron. Readjusting the leather straps holding my Itako certification and tools across my body, I sighed. It was always the same with her. Any handsome man, no matter his age, and she was trying to marry me off. Though I think she was overreaching with this one. Everyone in the region knew of Uesgugi Kenshin. There was no way he would be interested in marrying a blind shaman from a small village. I walked into the living room to sit at the low table.

Kagami settled down next to me, whispering in my mind. *My he is rather gorgeous. In another life I might have lured him into the forest and feasted on that hunk of beauty for days.*

It took so much willpower not to roll my eyes. Instead, I greeted Uesugi with a small bow of my head. A slight rustle and a clink of armor let me know the general position of the guard in the corner of our small room.

"I'm Yumi, the Itako," I unclipped the wooden box from around my waist and placed it on the ground in front of me, "What service can I provide you?"

"You're the Itako?" I heard the slosh of liquid in a tankard as he took a big swig of its contents.

"Yes," I said simply.

Travelers would often give this reaction, expecting me to be old and wrinkled or young but ugly. It's never stated, but there is strong prejudice around the blind, and most think that the ability to see and beauty are strongly linked, when in fact the two are not mutually exclusive.

"What is troubling you?" I pressed.

"It's... my daughter Shirayuki. She ... well I don't know... I need advice from ... umm... well..." another slosh signaled him taking another drink let me know he was trying to find liquid courage.

I figured I should rescue him from his stammering. He was clearly uncomfortable, but I was a bit puzzled. Standing over the place I judged Uesugi Kenshin to be was a spirit of a man with worry in his eyes and something else I couldn't place.

"I would suggest consulting your late wife, but I'm pretty sure you've never married, which begs the question of how you got a daughter," I mumbled the last part under my breath. It wasn't unheard of for a Daimyō to have concubines and conquests, though it was strange how involved he was in his illegitimate daughter's life if that was the case. Pushing these thoughts aside, I continued, "There is someone here who seems to have some stake in the matter, though I would think he is too young to be your father. A brother perhaps?"

There was a long pause. Uesugi Kenshin gulped down another drink.

The guard coughed, whether at my bluntness—I'd lost my desire for politeness over the years. Many dismissed my rudeness as a side effect for spending my time communing with the dead — or at Kenshin's drinking, I did not know.

"Brother..." Uesugi Kenshin finally spoke, his voice heavy with emotion, "I suppose I could call him that. Um, I guess I misspoke, Shirayuki, my adopted daughter, is his. His name is Shingen. He was a dear friend and left her to me to raise when he died about three years ago."

"Shingen. Takeda Shingen? The Tiger of Kai?" I asked.

"Is that so unbelievable?" This voice was different from Uesugi Kenshin's. Younger, more boyish, coming from the corner of the room where I imagined the guard stood. "When it's Uesugi

Kenshin sitting in front of you? The Dragon of Echigo."

"Point taken," I said, "Her mother wasn't around then I suppose?"

"No, she died in childbirth," Kenshin confirmed.

I nodded.

"What do you wish to ask?"

"What can I do to help her?"

I looked to the man standing across from me and opened my mouth. His words poured out of me. They were the words of a loving father and a dear friend. They told him not to worry, and to just be there and support her. But to also be firm and set boundaries. That it wasn't his fault, and that he didn't think he was a failure. That he was the best father she could have now that he was gone.

When he was done speaking I lurched forward. Usually, I would need a ritual to commune with the dead like that. But he was so ready, right there, I didn't need to call him over from the spirit realm.

I took an unsteady breath and pushed myself back into an upright position.

Uesugi Kenshin sniffed, and I wondered if

there were tears in his eyes. He took another drink before he spoke.

"Yumi," he said finally, "thank you."

"It is my pleasure," I bowed my head in respect.

"Um, do you mind me asking..." The guard's voice said from the corner, "how.... well.... how did you do it?"

"I'm sure you know the basics of how an Itako is trained, we are taught to recognize spiritual energy in our surroundings and channel or even manipulate it to do what we need it to do."

"Right but... he... you answered so quickly, I've never seen something done with so little..." he trailed off, trying to find the words that wouldn't sound offensive I suppose.

"Performance?" I smiled. "Well, it's not always so easy, but he was there waiting to speak with Mr. Uesugi. So, I didn't bother with the ritual. I had no spirit to summon. He was already there. And, well, I suppose I have a secret helper when it comes to channeling spirits." Kagami sighed in contentment as I stroked her head. She always lent her strength when it came to communing with the spirit realm, and she loved it when I praised her.

You should tell him it was me. I can appear as a Visage of beauty for him to grovel at. He is very handsome, I would quite like that.

I felt Kagami's longing to have this fantasy of hers played out so strongly it was as if it was my own desire. I gritted my teeth against the onslaught of her emotions as she communicated her desire to me.

Kagami... I chided, *no manipulating our customers...*

I heard Uesugi Kenshin shift where he was sitting and take another drink. The poor guy was a wreck.

Seriously though, aren't you even a little curious? Don't you want me to give you a peek at how handsome he is?

I tried to keep my face neutral as I argued with Kagami.

No, I'm not. I did my job, and we are going to get paid and I'll never hear from him again and that will be that. I don't need to see —

"Are there any more spirits here?" His voice pulled me out of my argument with Kagami just as an image flashed before my eyes of the men before me.

I caught my breath. The image was focused on

the man sitting across from me. His hair was pitch black and pulled into a messy ponytail, his features were petite and feminine and strangely alluring. His jaw was tense as he leaned closer to me. But what really caught my eye was the young samurai boy who stood behind him.

The guard was lean and rested against the wall, his hand resting on the hilt of his sword. It wasn't his appearance that struck me though, it was how he regarded me. He wasn't indifferent or upset that he had to talk to someone as low a station as me. He looked at me with interest and curiosity burning in his eyes. His eyes, a brown so deep they could have been black. I could have gotten lost in that blackness forever as it called to me with the question in his eyes. A question. They had asked me a question.

The image faded and my vision took a moment to adjust to the faint light streaming in from the windows and the blurry shadowy forms of the room's shadows and its occupants. I blinked, reorienting myself. I was so stunned I had forgotten what he had asked. I faintly realized my jaw had dropped.

A hand gently touched my shoulder, and I flinched.

"What?" I asked, surprised.

"Are you alright?" the guard asked.

"Yes!" My voice came out as a squeak.

"Were you... can you... were, umm..." I could hear him working his jaw more, but he didn't seem to be able to form his question.

Usually, I'm rather good at knowing what people are trying to say behind all their squeamishness around death and spirits, but I was too flustered and turned around to think straight so I simply said. "I'm sorry, I have a friend who likes to distract me. Um, no. There are no other spirits here." Kagami let out a yip and clamped her jaw disapprovingly before settling her head back on my lap.

"Oh, that's fine. I was just curious," his voice trailed off.

After a moment, one of them cleared their throat and the hand abruptly left my shoulder, leaving it cold.

"Will this be enough for your services?" Uesugi Kenshin asked.

He dropped a small purse full of coins in my hand. I knew by the weight of it that it was more than three times what I normally get, but I opened it and fingered the coins inside, judging the amount thoughtfully.

"Yes, this is enough, thank you," I bowed and then got up and walked to the front door, sliding the paper screen open for him as he and his guard joined me at the threshold.

"Thank you again for everything," he said.

I bowed again, telling him it was my pleasure and slid the door closed behind them.

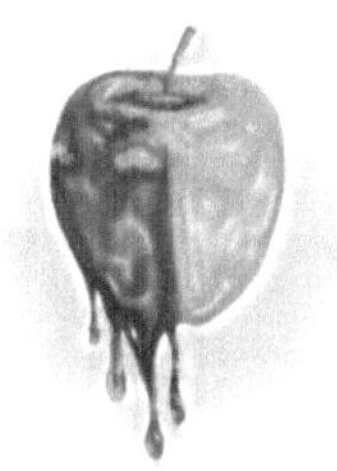

Chapter 11
The Proposal

The days passed slowly after that. I had mistakenly thought that now I was happy. I had a friend, and I was contributing to society with a job that I actually enjoyed. My mother was less stressed now that I had found my way in the world, and we were actually getting along for the most part. But now that I had met Uesugi Kenshin, I couldn't get him and his situation out of my head. My days were spent thinking of our meeting.

How kind and caring he seemed and how much weight he carried. He loved his daughter fiercely. Even though she wasn't his, he still wanted what was best for her and agonized over how to best parent her. But most of all, he was sad. He missed his friend. My heart would break a little thinking of how close they must have been for his friend to stay by his side even in the afterlife. And though I tried not to admit it, I spent more time than I should thinking of his guard. I couldn't get the image Kagami projected to me out of my head.

Often she would find me sighing over the image and give me a snarky comment about how she knew I wanted a peek at the handsome Uesugi Kenshin. Though I never admitted that it was the guard behind him that had me swooning.

More clients came and went. They always left satisfied, and yet, it left me feeling hollow. I wasn't enjoying my life. I simply floated along and let it happen to me. My purpose seemed trivial; solving the town's minor inconveniences with simple rituals. I realized that while I was respected for my skill as an Itako I would never have a friend who would care for me as Kenshin cared for his family. And no, Kagami doesn't count. While she is dear to me, she lacks human empathy to truly care that deeply for me. She would be terribly offended by that, but despite her being completely loyal and my dearest friend, I knew there were things she just couldn't wrap her head around. Complex human emotions was one of them. She, being an immortal being, doesn't quite get us humans, no matter how much time she spends with us.

I was thinking about Uesugi Kenshin while walking home from the town square —wondering how he and his daughter were getting on, doing my best to not let my thoughts wander to his guard—when I ran straight into a large form and fell smack on my butt.

I scrambled to my feet and bowed, "Forgive me. I didn't hear you coming. I was distracted. I'm so sorry."

A rich laugh tickled my ears, "Don't worry about it. I was actually getting up the courage to speak with you when I saw you round the corner and I... Well, I think I'm as much to blame as you." Uesugi Kenshin's commanding, albeit slightly raspy, voice bounded around in my head and I froze, stuck in a bow.

Kagami nudged my leg, and I forced myself to take a deep breath and bend the rest of the way down to pick up my scattered packages.

He is nervous, Kagami noted.

I reached out my hand to search for the packages when one was placed in it.

"Here, you can carry this one. I'll get the rest," Uesugi's guard said, and I heard him shift the boxes in his arms as he gathered them up.

Heat rose to my cheeks when I recognized his voice.

"Oh, thank you, but I'm really fine, you needn't trouble yourself." I reached out to take the packages from him.

"Nonsense, we're heading towards your house anyway."

"Yes," Uesugi Kenshin said after a long swig from his tankard, "we can talk on the way, it's actually the only reason I came back here."

"Oh. Okay," I began walking home, their footsteps falling in beside me. "So, what did you want to ask me?"

I glanced over in the direction of their footfalls and saw the form of Shingen hovering there.

"Did you want to speak with Shingen again?" I asked, trying to fill the silence.

Uesugi Kenshin paused another moment before saying, "oh no, well, no that's not why I'm here. Unless, well, does he have something to say?" He sounded so desperate I could hardly imagine this man commanding armies, but I suppose I only ever saw people's vulnerable side. I looked at Shingen and he just nodded. Understanding passed between us.

"He just says you're doing great, and he supports you. And that he believes you will do what's best for Shirayuki. That's why he left her to you."

Uesugi Kenshin was silent a long time after that. Aside from his footsteps and the slosh of his drink, I would have thought he stopped walking alongside me.

Ugh. Kagami said eventually. *This is too easy. He is so sensitive. Never mind Yumi. You can have him. I like at least a little bit of a challenge.*

You were never going to have him. I tell her. *You can't claim people Kagami, we've talked about this.*

Kagami snorted. *Well, I know you certainly have talked, but I still think it's a wonderful idea. As long as they put up a good fight. The game is no fun if you win too easily.*

I rolled my eyes. It was useless trying to talk sense into Kagami when she started daydreaming about taking the life force out of young strapping men. As long as she wasn't going to go off and do it, I let her dream.

"I'm sorry," Uesugi Kenshin's voice was ragged when he finally spoke. He cleared his throat and tried again. "I got lost for a moment there. Um, thank you for that, but it's not what I came here to ask."

"Right, of course, how else can I help?"

"I was hoping you would read my mind again so I wouldn't have to ask," he sighed.

A smile tugged at my lips, "unfortunately I don't read minds. I can read auras and see spirits, and that makes me a little more perceptive, but... well you might have noticed I'm less perceptive than usual today."

I waved my hand back to where we came from, indicating our run-in we had just a few minutes prior.

I heard his guard shift the parcels he was carrying for me.

"Has anyone told you that you blame yourself too much?" the guard asked.

I stalled my next step, stunned.

Blinking, I kept walking.

"Umm, no."

"Well, you do. It's not always your fault if you bump into someone. I can't count the times I've bumped into people because I wasn't paying attention to where I was going, but half the time it wasn't me, it was them and I-." he cut his sentence off abruptly, but I knew why.

Most people tiptoed around my blindness, thinking if they ever were to acknowledge it, that I would be dearly offended. Which, of course, is ridiculous.

"I know," I mumbled.

The silence stretched on some more. We were almost to my home. I figured Mr. Uesugi would have an even harder time getting his words out with my mother hovering, so I decided to give it my best guess.

"I can't bring him back. That's not within my power, and I wouldn't recommend seeking out a necromancer strong enough either. It wouldn't be him, not really."

"Oh! No! That's not. No." He sighed and mumbled to himself. "I was hoping, well, wondering, if you ever thought of moving?"

"I mean, eventually I suppose I might, but no..." I spoke slowly trying to understand what he was getting at.

He slowed his steps, and I looked around to find the dark shape of a house with candlelight flickering in the blurry windows. We had reached my home.

I heard them set the packages down on the

porch before settling next to them. I heard the slosh of his tankard again. The faint smell of alcohol filled my nose as he lifted it to drink.

"I don't want you to misunderstand my intentions. It's just, Shirayuki. She needs guidance, I can't give her that when I'm away at war. And I thought, well…" he took a swig of his drink, and it sloshed in the bottle.

"Don't you have staff, a nanny?"

"Yes… but they have too much sympathy for her. I need someone who won't be afraid to speak their mind. Someone who is kind and understanding but firm and perhaps a little intimidating. Someone like you."

I heard Kagami laughing in my head and it bounced around along with his words. She snorted and rolled onto her side knocking her back into my feet, almost knocking me over. Kenshin didn't comment on this; he simply took another drink.

"You want me to…"

"Be her mother."

There was a pounding in my ears as all the blood seemed to rush from my head. And yet heat was crawling up my neck. I felt like the world was tilting around me. The silence was filled with the pounding of our hearts, his from anxiety, and mine disbelief.

"Are you asking me to be your bride?" I finally blurted the words out.

"Wha-" he spluttered, choking on his latest swig of alcohol.

I rushed to explain. "I don't know Uesugi. I've never met your daughter. I don't know if I could mother her, I'm barely 16, I... I'm not ready for... I don't think I would make a good wife or mother."

"No, no you misunderstand, I'm not looking for a wife, just a mother for Shirayuki."

My mouth fell open. Heat rose into my cheeks and my face burned with embarrassment. I meant that I didn't think I was ready for marriage, regardless of what my mother would say. Even though I was relieved, it still stung when he said he didn't want me.

"Not that you wouldn't be a lovely wife," Uesugi Kenshin started backpedaling, "you're beautiful and I like you, I do, it's just I'm not in the market for one."

"No, it's fine you don't need to expla-"

"But I do," he cut me off, "see, I'm a devout Buddhist- I vowed not to marry."

"Oh." The stab of embarrassment in my heart lessened as he said that, "OH! That makes so much sense. That's why you never married."

He seemed to relax a little more and took another drink, the liquid sloshing as he tilted the bottle back.

"What I'm suggesting is not a marriage proposal, just that you'll come live at my castle and be part of the staff. You'll be the resident Itako for us and the surrounding area, and you will be a mother and friend to Shirayuki."

I was silent for a bit, trying to think through my embarrassment, and even more so wondering why the guard was being so silent. I wanted to know what he thought of this entire exchange.

Uesugi Kenshin rushed to fill the silence. "You would be well cared for, my city would greatly benefit from having such a powerful Itako nearby, and you can have all the finest kimonos or whatever you wish. I am a Daimyō, so I won't always be around to keep you company, but my maid servants are the best of the best and they will make sure you are well cared for in my absence when I must lead the fight."

I had been secretly thinking about the Uesugi family, hoping to see them again. Hoping I could hear *his* voice again, the guard who still hadn't commented on this exchange. But I didn't actually believe Uesugi Kenshin would come back, let alone ask me to live with him. But I would be crazy to go with him. I didn't know the first thing about being a good mother. And while the thought of living in a castle sounded amazing, could I really leave behind the only place I ever knew?

"I haven't been able to stop thinking about you," Uesugi continued to fill the silence. "You speak your mind and are honest. I think you and Shirayuki would get along nicely. I know you probably have many suitors and I don't want to get in the way of you having a chance to start a family of your own, but..." he trailed off.

I slowly sorted through his words, understanding finally pulling me out of my trance. "I have no suitors; no one in their right mind would want to marry me. I'm an Itako for one, my social status is that of a peasant, and on top of that I'm blind as a bat. Men either run for the hills when I pass or stand and gawk as I stumble about in the darkness so they can have a laugh. Why would a powerful Daimyō, who could hire the best nanny in the whole of Nihon, ask me, a blind girl you barely know, to be the mother to your adopted daughter?"

It was his turn to sit in stunned silence.

"I can't speak for any man but myself Yumi, but I would be a fool to let you spend the rest of your life here when I know you could help so many more people with your gifts in my city. And I honestly think you're exactly what Shirayuki needs right now."

I bit my lip and took a deep breath. "I don't know the first thing about being a mother," I said.

Uesugi Kenshin slugged another swallow of his drink before answering, "Mother is a strong word," he agreed, "I don't think she would appreciate a random woman coming in and trying to boss her around anyways. I would start with being her friend, a good influence, and maybe intimidate her a little so she will listen to you."

"Intimidate?" I asked.

"Don't worry you'll do that anyway, just be her friend."

"Is the great Uesugi Kenshin intimidated by a 16 year old blind girl?" I asked with a smile tugging at my lips.

"A 16 year old blind girl who is known across Nihon as one of the strongest Itako there is. Who walks around with a wild fox as a companion no less," he let out a small laugh before taking another swig and continued, "A little bit."

Fox!? Kagami practically shouted in my mind in outrage. *I'm a kitsune and quite a powerful one at that! Why if I-"*

"Shhh Kagami, settle." I didn't realize I spoke aloud at first, but I suppose it didn't matter. I stroked her head and soothed her raised shackles.

"A fox that doesn't like me apparently." Uesugi Kenshin noted, his drink sloshing more as he had to tilt it farther with each new swig.

I'm going to tell him. If he is going to let us live there he deserves to know what he is getting into. I tell Kagami.

Perfect. I'll show him intimidation. Kagami growled.

No, Kagami, you will behave.

You are absolutely no fun.

I sighed, "She actually liked you a little too much when she first saw you." I said. "There is something I need to tell you."

"Okay...."

"She isn't a fox, she is a kitsune."

I felt Kagami slightly shift and grow a few inches taller and begin to radiate heat.

"And I told you to behave," I chided Kagami.

"I'm behaving," she spoke aloud, "just thought he would like to see my true form.

Kagami's true form is what you'd expect. She is still a fox, she has the same red coloring and ink dipped ears and feet with a snow white chest and tail tips. Except bigger. Not huge mind you, but bigger than a little fox you'd find in the forest, and she has seven tails. Each one symbolizing a thousand years of life and each one adding to the power she is capable of.

Kagami sat next to my feet, her seven tails swishing gently along the ground, each other, and my leg.

It was the guard who spoke first.

His voice was smaller and quieter than before. "I'm not going to lie. I was not expecting that."

Uesugi Kenshin took another gulp of his drink.

I laughed. And eventually they joined me, hesitant at first, but eventually it felt natural.

When we quieted, I settled on the ground next to Kagami who, still showing off her seven tails, cuddled up on my lap. Her front paws and head resting on me and her ever moving swarm of tails brushing my arms and back as they moved. I sighed with contentment, but figured they needed more context.

"You should know she doesn't mean any harm. Well... no, she doesn't. She is very loyal to me, so if I ask her not to she won't bother anyone. But she does like to sneak out and play pranks on people at night. Mostly harmless stuff- she just makes them get lost and disoriented before helping them find their way out of the forest. It's not nice, but she also isn't, like, killing them or letting them wander forever helpless, so," I heaved a huge sigh, "I compromised and let her keep doing it."

They were silent for a long time before Uesugi Kenshin coughed, "Um. I was nodding, sorry you probably didn't notice, but I trust you. If you say she won't harm anyone, I believe you. She will be welcomed as your companion. Does she, um, will I need to ask the staff to have a suite set aside for her upon your arrival?"

Oh, I like him again, Kagami said to me.

But aloud she said, "I share my bed with Yumi, I wouldn't have it any other way."

Heat burned across my cheeks. "I... she means

that she is fine sharing with me, she isn't- We aren't-that close."

"Of course not Yumi," I could almost hear the laughter he was trying to hold in.

"I just wanted to make sure, I know kitsune have a reputation, and I just want to set the record straight. We never, I would never-"

Finally, Kagami put me out of my misery, "Oh you guys are too easy. This will be fun." She threw her head back, knocking my hand off, and laughed.

I took a deep breath to quell my temper. "Like I said. She likes to play harmless jokes."

"Yes, I imagine she will make life back home very interesting. It will be fun. Though I don't want to tell the staff about her. If you wish to tell Shirayuki, I'll leave that to your discretion. I'd wait to decide until you meet her, though."

"Of course, whatever you wish."

"So, you agree to come then? I'm sorry, I don't recall if you ever said yes."

"Yes, I'll come. As long as my parents are okay with it." I smiled.

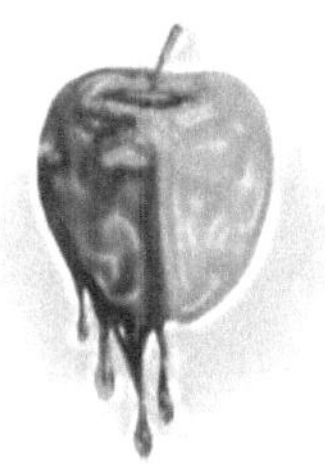

Chapter 12
Journey to Echigo Capital

I wasn't worried about my parents agreeing. My father will agree to anything when given enough logic and I say that it's what I want. And my mother would be happy to give me the opportunity to potentially get a man to fall in love with me, marry me, and raise our family's status. It helped that Uesugi Kenshin asked and made it sound more like an order as the ruling daimyō of our province.

I was being recruited to work in his court as an Itako. They couldn't very well turn down a direct order from our leader. My mother whisked me away and fixed my hair before ensuring I was packing all of the best beauty products we had and only my finest kimonos.

We arranged to leave at first light, so after packing I tried to sleep unsuccessfully.

***

When the first light of dawn began peeking through my window, I got dressed. Grabbed my packed bag, slung my bamboo over my head, and tied my wooden box of Itako tools around my waist and settled it into the small of my back. I lugged my bag to the living room and left it resting close to the front door. I began to pace, my stomach churning as I waited for Usegui to arrive with his caravan.

You are going to wear a hole in the floor, Kagami chided.

Would you rather I bite my nails? I shot back.

You're doing that too.

Crap. I pulled my hand down from my mouth and felt along my fingertips. Most of my nails were a jagged mess now. My mother would not be impressed.

What are you even worried about? Kagami pressed her body against my legs, and I leaned down to stroke her. She pressed her presence into my mind- on the edges of my vision I could see her bright orange and red light, and a calming warmth spread over me.

What if his staff doesn't like me? What if Shirayuki hates me? What if he changes his mind?

What if- I forced a wall up before my next thought automatically flowed to her. I took a deep breath.

They will like you because you're amazing. Shirayuki will admire you for how awesome I am, so by default you have to be cool too, and Usegui wouldn't do that.

How do you know?

Cuz even if you don't get along with anyone, he likes your company and values your abilities enough to not let you go. Also, he is scared of me.

Kagami, what did I tell you about reading people's minds?

That it's super fun?

I rolled my eyes and waited for a more appropriate answer.

Okay, you know what? Why don't you become a sentient all powerful fox spirit that is bound to the soul of a lovesick girl who just sits in her room all the time and tell me you never get bored. Kagami snapped at me, literally chomped her jaws in my face.

Ouch.

Well, it's true.

I'm not love sick.

Keep telling yourself that, Kagami quipped, *Besides you are missing the point, you need to make more friends, because then I'll have more friends.*

You mean you will have more people to snoop around in the heads of?

Exactly, you get it.

I gave an exasperated sigh and resumed my pacing. My mother came out of her room and started making breakfast. I decided to help to keep my mind off the fact that Kenshin and his guard weren't here yet. My father came out to eat and gave me a hug. He asked if I was all packed. I nodded, trying to force myself to swallow my food and sit still. I was just starting to clean up breakfast when finally, finally there was a knock on the door. My limbs froze, but my mother's gained superspeed and she ran to the door in record time and wrenched it open.

My father came and guided me to the door, giving me one last hug and telling me how proud he was of me. My head was reeling. The man at the door wasn't Kenshin or his guard, his voice was different.

"May I take your bags Miss Yumi?" He asked.

I nodded, trying to get words out and failing. I turned to where I'd left the bag, but my father rested a hand on my shoulder saying, "Yes, here it is." I heard the contents rustle as he passed it off to the man.

There was an awkward pause, "Any more?" he finally asked.

I shook my head, "That's all."

"Alright then, if you would follow me, Kenshin is waiting in the cart."

I hurried after him as his setta[16] scraped on the hard earth. I paused, hovering behind him when his footsteps stopped. He gave a small grunt, and I heard my bag land on something solid. The man bustled around a bit, and I assumed he was securing my bag in place for the road.

"Yumi!" Uesugi Kenshin's voice boomed, and I heard a thud as he jumped from the cart to greet me. "Are you well?"

"Yes," I bowed in respect, as is custom, but he grabbed my chin to keep my face from dipping any lower.

I stiffened at his touch.

"You are to be a member of my court, and the

---

[16] **Setta** /**seh**-tah/ traditional Japanese footwear resembling flip flops, with a smooth sole, more suitable for samurai.

mother of my child. There is no need for that." His words, how he phrased it, sent heat rushing to my cheeks. I had no desire to be known as the mother of his child, and here he was announcing it to the world. What happened to being friends and a good influence?

I straightened.

"Good, and since we are on the subject, drop the Uesugi, it's just Kenshin."

"Yes of course, Ues-" I had to stop myself from bowing and saying his surname. "Umm..-Kenshin," I finished.

"Are you ready for the journey?" his guard asked. Now I really wished I could bow to hide my face from the guard.

"Yes." I managed to squeak out before reaching out and running my hand along the side on the cart so I wouldn't run into it.

Interesting, Kagami mused in my mind, but I ignored her. I didn't have the will to stop whatever she thought was interesting at the moment. I just hoped it didn't embarrass me.

"Would you like help up? The step is a little high," The guard's voice, the one I recognized from before, was right next to me now. He sounded eager to help.

I found the step and turned to him, "Perhaps just a hand?"

I reached out in his direction, and he grasped my hand. I touched the step with my free hand, so I knew how high it was before lifting my foot up to the bottom step. I reached up for a hand hold and grabbed the edge of the cart to help pull myself up. Using the guard's hand for balance, I brought my other foot up to the high step. Once I was up, it was simple enough to climb the rest of the way unassisted. I felt around for the seat and settled down on the far end of the bench.

"Do you ride in carts often?" the guard asked.

I felt the frame tilt and creak as he and Kenshin climbed in after me.

I scoffed, "No."

"Right, it's just you seemed to know your way around."

"Well, I'm pretty good at adapting to my environment." I mumbled.

I heard the other guard climb onto the cart and the jingle of metal against metal, then a horse neigh. As Kagami settled down at my feet, the men jumped a little and the cart creaked.

"Oh my, I suppose she can just appear when she wants." Kenshin said, popping the cork from his bottle.

I reached down and patted Kagami, "Yes. Though I don't always realize when she isn't physically here. Sorry for the scare."

"Not a problem."

The new guard spoke from the front of the cart, "All set sir?"

"Yes, let's go."

There was another creak as the guard settled somewhere in front of the cart. A crack split through the air just before the cart lurched forward and the sound of thundering hooves reached my ears.

"The trip will take about three days by cart." Kenshin said after a while.

"Okay," I said.

He shifted and I heard the click of bottles as he retrieved one.

"Would you like a drink?" he asked.

He popped the cork, and I smelled a whiff of alcohol before it was whisked away with the wind.

I responded with a question before I could think better of it. "So, you're a devout Buddhist. Vowed not to marry, but you love to drink?"

Kenshin laughed, "I never said I was perfect."

The young guard spoke next, "Dad always had a weakness for some good saké. Nothing can get him to part with it. Even Shirayuki, and well, you know the lengths he will go for her."

I choked, "Sorry, did you say dad?"

"Um, yeah." The guard says, "I guess I never properly introduced myself. I'm Kagekatsu, Kenshin's eldest adopted son."

"So Shirayuki is your little sister?" I wanted to smack myself for asking such a dumb question.

"Well, technically. But me and my brother, Kagetora, we were adopted way before Shirayuki. We love her, but she can be a handful."

"Which is where I come in," I guessed.

"Don't get me wrong, it's not like she is completely off the rails or a big brat. She is just a little too invested in the war effort. At first we loved it. She actually trains a lot of our soldiers. Even though she's only 12 she's one of our best fighters. Her dad, Shingen, taught her the way of the sword from the moment she could walk. But, some of her battle tactics became... less than honorable. If that wasn't bad enough, she wanted to start experimenting with dark magic and..." Kagekatsu's voice trailed off.

"It's why I thought you would be a good fit to keep an eye on her," Kenshin paused to take a swig of his drink. "Especially with that um..- friend of yours. You could keep her safe, maybe stop her from going too far."

More liquid sloshed as he took another sip.

Fear filled their voices when they spoke of Shirayuki. It left me wondering what this young girl had gotten into that left these samurai warriors so worried.

Chapter 13
Meeting Shirayuki

We spent the three days of travel talking about their home, Shirayuki, their conquests, my gifts as an Itako, my childhood, and Kagekatsu's childhood and how he came to be one of Kenshin's adopted children. The other guard who manned the horses told me his story as well, how he came to be one of Kenshin's elite warriors and good friends. He was not the other son, but an old teacher and mentor whose name was Koga Tomotame.

We skirted around the topic of Kagami being a kitsune for the sake of Koga. But being her vain self, she loved being the center of attention, so she would often rub against one of them and beg to be petted if I wasn't giving her enough attention. At night we made camp and slept in a circle around the fire. Kagami curled up on my bedroll, keeping me warm.

Soon enough, the three days passed and we arrived at the Usegui estate. Kenshin was checking his supply of saké; the bottles clinked together as he sifted through them. I felt the cart groan as Kagekatsu jumped out. Before I had a chance to find the steps down, hands wrapped around my waist, lifting me down. When I was securely back on my feet, they released me.

"Sorry," Kagekatsu apologized, immediately, perhaps noticing the surprise on my face at being plucked up from the cart. "I wasn't thinking, I shouldn't have-"

"It's fine." I assured him before he rambled on for too much longer. I took a deep breath before I continued- trying to calm my racing heart. "It just took me by surprise. Maybe just next time ask first?" My voice went up an octave at the end of my question. Uncertain if I should even be saying it. He was the daimyō's son after all.

"Of course!" he said, "I'll do better at remembering that for next time."

Over the bustle of the servants arriving and unloading the cart I heard him turn on his heel, twisting the dirt with a scraping sound, and addressed a servant.

"Please prepare a suite for Yumi to rest and

send Shirayuki down if she isn't coming already." Light and quick footfalls hurried away, letting me know the servant hurried inside. It was soon hard to distinguish much as more servants came and began unloading the cart and unhitching the horses. But even with all the chaos I could hear around me, there was no mistaking the young girl shouting as loud as she could as she sprinted into Kenshin's arms.

"Uncle Kenshin!!!!" She yelled. "Uncle Kenshin, Uncle Kenshin you're baaaaaack!"

"Shirayuki!" Kenshin grunted as she ran full force into him, "My beautiful child, how are you!"

"My form is getting even better, do you want to see? Master Tsugaru tells me that I'll be better than you and papa soon!"

I smiled. I knew I was only four years older than Shirayuki, but she was so carefree and happy, I was expecting a hardened critic from the way Kenshin and Kagekatsu spoke of her. She was just an adorable kid though.

"No surprise there. You have the second best samurai blood running through your veins." Kenshin said.

"Whatever, you know papa could've totally taken you."

"I guess we will never find out, will we." Kenshin said, sadness creeping into his voice. The form of Shingen, Shirayuki's father, solidified around them. He looked at me with heartbreak in his eyes before fading back into the spirit realm.

There was a beat of silence, then Shriayuki's voice rang out, "Hey, can I show you what I've been working on? Maybe we can spar."

Kenshin laughed. "Maybe in a little bit okay? First I want you to meet Yumi." They shifted to face me, the ground scraping beneath their setta. "Shirayuki, this is Yumi, she is the best Itako in Nihon and I asked her to come be a part of the court because I think our city deserves only the best."

I gave her a wave and an awkward smile.

"She's blind" Shirayuki said flatly.

"Most Itako are," I chuckled.

"You have a pet fox?" She asked after a beat of silence.

"Yes, this is Kagami. Don't worry she's tame," I almost stopped there, but after thinking about it I added, "Mostly."

A small excited gasp escaped her lips.

I thought so, she likes danger. That's why she

is training to be a samurai. She wants to fight as much as Kenshin and her father did.

"Can she do any tricks?" Shirayuki asked.

I immediately felt a rush of anger that wasn't mine. I reached down and grabbed Kagami by the hackles and put all my strength into pulling her back.

Tricks? Oh, I can show you some tricks. Who do you think I am? Some common woodland creature? I'll show you what I can do. Come on Yumi, let me at her, the little demon.

"Okay enough!" I grunted as I gave one final pull and finally Kagami fell backward into me, the momentum pulling us both to the ground in a heap. Shirayuki's laughter filled my ears and mingled with Kagami's grumbling.

I took a few deep breaths and sat up. Loosely putting my arm across Kagami so I could stop her if needed.

Shirayuki's laughter soon ended.

"Kagami is quite prideful," I said. "She doesn't appreciate being compared to a regular house pet you could train, or, well, anything regular for that matter."

"She can understand what I'm saying?"

Shirayuki asked.

Kagami grumbled in my mind again but aloud she let out a low growl.

"Yes, she is quite intelligent."

Kenshin coughed. Perhaps worried I would tell Shirayuki about Kagami here where anyone would overhear, but I wasn't going to. I hadn't decided if that was a good idea yet.

"She is beautiful." Shirayuki breathed.

And Kagami's growl turned into, well, not a purr because canines don't purr, but as close as you could get to one. Kagami leaned away from me and I realized that Shirayuki had reached out to pet her and Kagami was leaning into the affection.

"Yes. She thinks so too." I said.

"Can you speak with her?" Shirayuki gasped, amazed.

I flinched, "I'm an Itako. I can speak with the dead. Is it so far-fetched that I can speak to my companion?"

"Wow." Shirayuki breathed. "What does she think of me?"

"Hmmm...."

This girl is two sides of the same coin, happy and pleasant one minute and deadly serious the next. She is also very calculating and manipulative. Tell her I think she is clever, strong and brave.

"She says she thinks you're clever, strong and brave... and you give good pets" I added with a laugh.

Shirayuki's laughter joined mine, and I heard Kenshin let out a sigh.

"I wonder how effective she could be on the battlefield," she mumbled to herself as if calculating the possibilities.

I could bring your armies to their knees with barely a thought. Kagami swelled with pride.

I gave an uneasy laugh, "I think it's best if we don't find out."

"Hmmm... do you want to see the castle? I'll give you a tour and then you and Kagami can watch me spar with Uncle Kenshin!" Shirayuki was already grabbing my hand and pulling me up, not recognizing that I wouldn't be 'watching' much of anything.

"You two run along. I'll meet you in the training room. I have to speak with Ujie." Kenshin called after us.

"Ujie doesn't know a thing about warfare, you're wasting your time" Shirayuki mumbled under her breath.

I got a speed run tour that still lasted close to an hour. The castle was huge. Shirayuki asked a passing servant which suite would be mine and walked me there. The servants were just finishing up preparing the suite, so Shirayuki politely asked if they would draw a bath for me so I could wash after I 'watched' her spar with Kenshin. And to draw one for her as well.

Eventually, we made it to the training room. I was pretty turned around, but I knew Kagami could always tell me which way I would need to go if I wound up lost without a guide.

The training room was a big open space with wooden floors. Shirayuki took me to the far wall so I could run my hand along the wooden training swords she would be using momentarily, and she told me that the rest of the walls were lined similarly with either wooden practice swords or spare samurai swords.

I asked her if she had a favorite and she gently placed a small slim metal contraption in my hand. Upon further investigation I realized it was a fan, just made of metal.

"My father made it for me before he passed. It's white with red cherry blossoms decorating it, but when it's closed it's just plain black" she explained.

I ran my hand along the cool metal, confused why she would show me this when I asked about weapons.

"It's a tessen," she continued when she noticed my confusion, "my father fought with one and trained me to as well. It's great for defense, but I still learned sword fighting as well. I usually will dual wield the tessen, or a katana[17] and a tessen, occasionally just the katana, if I'm not worried about the opponent."

She gently plucked the fan from my hands, folding the metal sheets with a *shink* of metal collapsing together. Then she placed a sheathed sword in my hands. The wood was cool and very smooth. The handle was braided with leather.

"It's blood red with a black leather handle. The blade is black, with a little white entwined . It's one of a kind. Kenshin made it for me when I was little. My name, Shirayuki, means snow white, my mother gave it to me for my pale complexion before she died soon after I was born, but Kenshin made this

---

[17] **Katana** /**kah**-tah-na/ a long, curved single-edged sword traditionally used by Japanese samurai.

to match my hair and lips."

I realized that we had something in common. We were both named for our looks. We both naturally looked like the beauty standard across Nihon. I kept quiet though. It wasn't something she would have wanted to hear, and it was just pointing out the obvious to someone who could have looked and seen the connection right away.

"Alright Shirayuki," Kenshin's voice rang through the training room, "you ready for me to wipe the floor with you?"

Shirayuki took the sword back from me and placed it back on the wall.

"Yeah right, you're getting slow in your old age uncle. I think I'll beat you yet."

Kenshin laughed, "Not today young one. Not today."

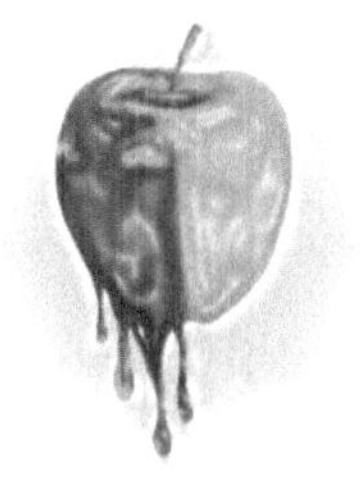

Chapter 14
Eavesdropping

There was silence and then a loud crack as their wooden swords met. They sparred for a while until one of their swords clattered to the ground.

Shirayuki groaned in frustration and said, "Again."

Clack! Their swords met.

This went on for a while. I sat at the edge of the room waiting and listening to the sounds of their fight.

Shirayuki is quite skilled, Kagami informed me, *but Kenshin is in a league all his own. He could end these a lot faster than he is, but he is instead going out of his way to create opportunities for her to go on the offensive. Once he has done that a couple times, he kicks into high gear and disarms her and corners her in seconds. Still, I wouldn't be surprised if she was the best Samurai in this compound aside from him, her skill is impressive.*

When Shirayuki is panting and exhaustedly calling that they go again, Kenshin insists that it is time to get cleaned up for dinner, and we go our separate ways.

After a nice relaxing bath, I dress in my favorite kimono and rest my bamboo across my back. I don't bother with my box of Itako tools as I'm not leaving the castle, I simply place it on the desk in the corner of my room.

As I slide open my door, I hear the rustle of a kimono being straightened and hurried footsteps.

"Yumi!" Kenshin said, "can I talk with you about Shirayuki?"

"Um, sure?"

"How are you getting along?"

"Pretty good, I think Kagami made a good impression at least." Kagami pressed against my leg and I leaned down to rest my hand on her head.

"Yes, she wasn't as intimidated by you as I hoped..."

"Well that is a relief. I do hope we can be

friends, and that would be hard if she were afraid of me."

"And what about," Kenshin shifted uncomfortably, "her tendency for war and being stronger?"

I opened my mouth but then paused, thinking about it.

Shirayuki is eavesdropping. Kagami said in a sing-song voice in my mind.

"I think," I pressed my lips together, "I think that she doesn't think you give her enough credit. She has great ideas and wants to support your war efforts. She pushes to be in your inner circle and know what's going on. After all, her father died in the war. I doubt she wants to lose you too."

It wasn't what he asked, but it's what Shirayuki would be most okay hearing. It was the truth, and Kenshin needed to know it, but it also put me in a position of having her back. I needed her to trust that I wasn't only here to spy on her for him.

"She is definitely at war in her own self as much as our country," he murmured, then added, "And you think you will get on okay when I'm gone?"

I sighed, "I think if you want your daughter's opinion of me, you should ask her. As far as me getting along with everyone at the castle when you have to leave again, I think I'll be able to make a friend or two. I don't have the most practice at making friends, but I'll manage."

Please, please, stop asking about Shirayuki, I silently pleaded. It would make things worse if she knew that he wanted me to be a surrogate mother to her. I didn't want to be a mom. I would befriend her and advise her to make better choices and be a good influence, but I am not going to mother her. We had talked about this on the ride here. He agreed that he thought she wouldn't resist a friend as much as a mother.

He grunted, "Are you settled in okay?"

"Yes, thank you," I breathed a sigh of relief.

"Would you like me to show you the way to the dining hall? I don't want to keep Shirayuki waiting too long."

"That would be great."

As we walked, Kagami spoke to me.

You're playing a dangerous game, Yumi. You cannot be both her mother and her friend.

I do not wish to replace her mother. I said.

No, but you do need to be an authority figure.

I know, but I can still be friendly with her.

Just don't lean too hard into friendship. When the time comes to step up and take charge, it will be so much harder.

"Yumi?" Kenshin's voice pulled me out of my thoughts with Kagami.

"Hmm?" I asked, distracted.

"I just said we are here and your seat is just to your left."

"Oh, thanks." I lowered myself down onto a cushion next to the low table.

Dinner was filled with Kenshin, Kagekatsu, and Kagetora chatting about the war effort, which fascinated Shirayuki. She even gave them advice about various routes and strategies to use. Occasionally Kagekatsu would try to include me in the conversation, but for the most part I spent the evening quietly listening, learning the family's dynamic.

Chapter 15
Necromancy

The days passed quickly, and soon it felt like I was a part of the family. Even Kagetora warmed up to me, despite me making him nervous. Shirayuki and I, much to Kenshin's delight, became fast friends. She was fascinated by my powers and how I 'trained' Kagami.

One day I was combing the tangles out of her hair when she asked if I could control the dead. I knew this was coming of course, thanks to Kagami's bad habit of mind reading. I was explaining the difference between an Itako, who simply communes with the dead and casts out evil spirits, and a necromancer, who can raise corpses and command them, when I mentioned my master was a necromancer.

Shirayuki immediately perked up. "You were

trained by a necromancer?"

"Yes."

"Why didn't he teach you necromancy instead?" She asked incredulously.

"Because he got into necromancy to bring back the family he had lost when he was just a boy, and the process drove him a little mad. They looked like his family, but they were just empty shells waiting to be filled with his will or to finally be put to rest. Eventually he realized that it wasn't healthy, and it wasn't fair to his dead family to not let them be at rest, so he swore off necromancy."

"So he didn't teach you because of his own weak constitution," Shirayuki concluded.

I laughed more at how she spoke her blunt remark than the meaning behind it. At this point I had gotten all the tangles out of her hair and was doing long strokes with the brush to distribute the oils on her head to the ends to make it shine.

"I suppose you could look at it like that. But there was another, more apparent reason. While vision isn't a requirement for necromancy, it certainly would be almost impossible without it. Without seeing what your target is doing, or their surroundings, it makes it rather difficult to give them commands."

"I suppose that makes sense…" Shirayuki paused, thinking. "Would you have to be the one to give them commands, or could you tell them to heed the direction of someone else?"

"I never thought to ask. Though I suppose that should work in theory."

"I wish we could test it out," she said wistfully. "Could you imagine an army of the dead under our control? We would be unstoppable. The look on the enemy's face as they cut down a soldier just to see its corpse rise and keep fighting, priceless."

"The only problem is getting a necromancer who could control that many," I said, gently trying to dissuade the idea without upsetting her.

"Hmm, how many could your master control?"

"He was very strong, he could control five at a time without a problem. Add any more and he would risk passing out."

"You're right, that's not very practical to have enough necromancers to make a difference." Shirayuki reached up and ran her fingers through her hair that now felt like silk. "You are very good at this. Did you do your own hair as well?"

"Yes, my mother made sure I could take care of my own hair and put it up from a young age."

"I've always hated getting my hair brushed by the maids and nannies growing up. It was always a tangled mess, but you were very gentle."

I smiled at the compliment, "It probably wouldn't get so tangled if you tied it up more."

"Can you blame me? By the time they are through with the brushing, there is no way I wanted to sit through any more torture!"

"Would you like me to have a go at it?" I asked. "Or, I can teach you how to do it yourself."

"Yes! Please!"

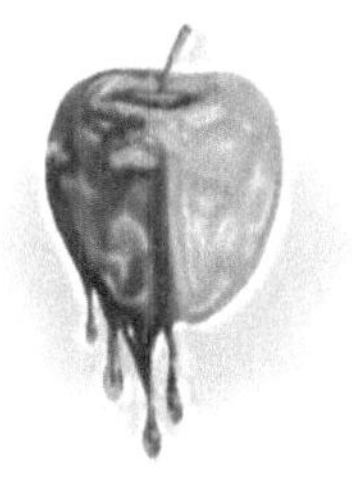

Chapter 16
An Outing

One morning, as summer was giving way to fall with cooler nights, Shirayuki appeared at my bedroom door when I was on my way to breakfast.

"Uncle Kenshin is coming back today!" She practically exploded with excitement. Her bare feet danced along the wooden floor as she paraded around me.

"How do you know?" I asked.

"He sent a message ahead to tell me, it arrived late last night."

I tried to control the fluttering in my stomach. If Kenshin was returning, then there was a good chance that Kagekatsu would as well.

Kagami pressed her body against my leg for attention. *You have it worse than Ujie Yasutoshi does for Shirayuki.*

I ignored the comment but absently leaned to scratch behind her ears. Sir Ujie was a young guard, maybe 13 or 14 years old, who was completely smitten with Shirayuki.

"Oh, hey Kagami, where have you been?" Shirayuki bent down to hug my fox demon.

"She has been exploring the palace and probably causing mischief," I said.

"Aww, she could never cause any mischief! She is such a good girl. Aren't you Kagami?" I heard a thud and I assumed Kagami and Shirayuki settled on the ground so Kagami could receive belly rubs.

Yeah Yumi, I could NEVER cause any mischief, Kagami said smugly.

I snorted, "Oh you would be surprised."

Once Shirayuki had sufficiently fawned over Kagami, she said, "So, I have been meaning to go into town, do you want to come? We have to leave now so we get back before Uncle Kenshin."

"Sure!" I said. "What guard did you get to agree to accompany us?"

"Ugh, do we have to bring a guard? Can't you see how pointless that is? I train most of them. I'm better at protecting myself than they ever could be! Kenshin and his boys get to gallivant across the country and I'm stuck in this stuffy old house! I could be a general by now, but Kenshin will never hear of it!" A loud thud reverberating through the floor tells me she punctuated the point by punching the ground. She took a deep breath and stood up, her kimono rustling as she calmed her tempter. "You see how unfair that is, right?"

"No, I can't see," I nudged her arm and smiled. "But I do understand your frustration. Still, what harm does bringing a guard along do?"

"Other than the fact that it is degrading that he thinks I need protection from a useless guard that I can beat in less than a minute?" she grumbled.

"Yes, other than that."

"I think it's stupid for him to keep one of his best fighters and strategists on the sidelines."

I didn't respond. I didn't know how to tell her his reasons went beyond protecting his dear friend's child. That he was worried if he put her in the thick of the war she wouldn't be the same. That bloodlust would take over and she wouldn't be bringing honor to her family name any more, but disgrace.

"He wastes valuable time coming back here to consult me and spend time with me. Now that it is fall, I doubt he will go out again till spring. It's no wonder he hasn't finished this yet."

I decided a subject change was in order. "I don't think you're talking about going out shopping any more," I quipped.

"Ugh, Yumi!" she complained. "Don't you have a heart! Can't you tell how humiliating it is for me to always be accompanied by a guard! You know Akina would let me go," She ventured.

That's when I stopped trying to be nice and understanding. I stiffened and stormed right up to her. Akina was her nanny most of her time here and Shirayuki liked to manipulate her to get what she wanted. The last time Akina had tried to talk Shirayuki out of something unsuccessfully, Akina almost lost her job. I liked Akina. I told General Koga to officially make me Shirayuki's new nanny and assign Akina elsewhere so that wouldn't happen again.

"And when Kenshin found out that you went out unsupervised and Akina let you go, who did he punish?" I yelled in her face, my fists clenched tight at my sides.

Shirayuki scoffed and pushed passed me.

"Akina had to work three weeks without pay," I told her. "Her children went hungry for three weeks. All because you were selfish and went out on the town without a guard and when Kenshin found out, you told him Akina let you go."

"That's her own fault," Shirayuki mumbled.

"No. That's your fault. She did what you asked after you threatened to have her fired. That's blackmail. If it was her fault, then you're saying she should have made you stay home. Is that what you're saying?"

"No." Shirayuki's voice was barely a whisper.

We were both silent for a while after that. Finally, Kagami whined and nudged my leg. *Wow you almost sound like a parent.*

Oh shut up!

I sighed and tried to smooth my facial expressions. "Come on, let's go find a guard so we can hurry and be back before Kenshin arrives." I linked my arm through hers and began pulling her towards the main courtyard. "Think of it as a training exercise for them. Who do you think needs it the most?"

That helped smooth over her temper.

"Definitely Sir Ujie," she said.

And we hurried off to find him.

Chapter 17
Lost Princess

Shirayuki thoroughly enjoyed turning our outing into training the poor guard. I honestly felt a little bad for him when he eagerly agreed to accompany her into the city. He probably was hoping the quality time could be spent trying to woo her. Instead, she spent every spare moment drilling him on not paying attention to his surroundings enough, or not keeping a close enough eye on his charge. Once she even slipped away from us. Sir Ujie was a mess when he realized she was missing.

We —and I use that term loosely, as I wasn't much help— looked for her for over an hour with no luck. I spent that entire time trying not to get lost myself. I knew my way around town pretty well. I've done house calls as part of my duties as an Itako, I knew I would most likely be able to find my way back home, but that wouldn't help if Sir Ujie and

Shirayuki didn't look for me there. I followed closely behind Sir Ujie and followed the sounds of his shouts if we got separated in a crowd, which happened often. I couldn't rely on Kagami to guide me, because I sent her off to search the city for Shirayuki once she disappeared and it became apparent that Ujie would have little luck finding her on his own.

Shirayuki was right about one thing: Ujie definitely needed more training in guarding someone. He was so worried about Shirayuki he lost all sense of what was going on around him.

I trailed behind his line of destruction as he plowed past people, calling for Shirayuki. People grumbled when I passed that the boy needed to look where he was going. I was beginning to think Shirayuki chose him to be her guard specifically so she could ditch him. This was made increasingly more obvious as the search dragged on.

Finally, Kagami's voice rang in my ears, *I found her.*

I stopped in my tracks. *Where?*

In a run-down old shop advertising magical items. It's south-east of the main square where we lost her.

Watch her!

Obviously.

"Sir Ujie!" I yelled.

No response.

I chastised myself for not grabbing his attention sooner, he was likely long gone now.

I reached out until I found someone's arm.

"Excuse me!" a man's voice said accusingly. "Watch where you're going!"

"I'm so sorry, but have you seen a young man in a guard's uniform running around and shouting for a Shirayuki?"

"Yeah, he went that way, now if you'll-"

"That way?" I interrupted before he could flee the exchange, pointing in a random direction.

"No! I said that way!"

I took a deep breath. "Can you please point my arm in the right direction?"

"What in the blazes are you on about? I told you where he went. Now stop playing games!"

"Argh!" I shouted, frustrated with the grouchy man. I released him and turned to find someone else to ask.

Reaching out again my hand brushed someone's kimono so I grabbed it and gave it a tug.

"So sorry but have you seen a young boy in a guard's uniform running around?"

"Yumi, there you are!" Sir Ujie said.

I gave a little jump in surprise at hearing his voice.

"I still haven't found Shirayuki and then I turned around and you were gone and oh, Kenshin is going to kill me!"

"I know where Shirayuki is," I said once he finally took a breath.

"What, where?"

"At an old shop south east of the main square."

Sir Ujie reached out and squeezed my arm. "You're amazing!" he said before releasing me and running off through the crowd.

"Great," I said as I tried to navigate through the crowd and listen for Sir Ujie, hoping I was going the correct way.

After a while of dodging past people and completely losing any idea of where Sir Ujie ran off to, I was lost in a sea of bodies and a cacophony of noise. Between children laughing, babies crying, the thrum of the shoppers' feet, and the shouts of shopkeepers, I lost hope of picking up Ujie's trail.

Wait there, I see you, Kagami said.

I heaved a sigh of relief and stepped to the side so I was out of foot traffic. I waited for Kagami to reach me.

Do you have Shirayuki with you? I asked while I waited.

Yes, once she was done at the magic shop I intercepted her and she happily is following me. Where's Ujie?

I was hoping he was with you. What was Shirayuki doing unsupervised?

She bought a book on dark magic. She thinks I didn't see her until the shop was out of sight. The book is hiding in the folds of her kimono.

Thanks.

Of course! Can I read her mind to find out why she is looking into magic?

No, let me talk to her in private first.

"Yumi! There you are!" Shirayuki's voice rang out above the bustling crowd.

"Shirayuki!" Sir Ujie bellowed from behind me.

"I am so sorry! You were right! I'm a terrible guard! Please forgive me and continue to teach me!"

Footsteps barreled past me and I could just hear the clink of his sword against his belt over the bustle of crowd around us as he stopped in front of me. His tall frame blocked sunlight from my field of vision before it suddenly sunk to the ground.

"Oh get up Ujie," Shirayuki laughed. "No need to cause a scene. Of course I will continue your training, you desperately need it."

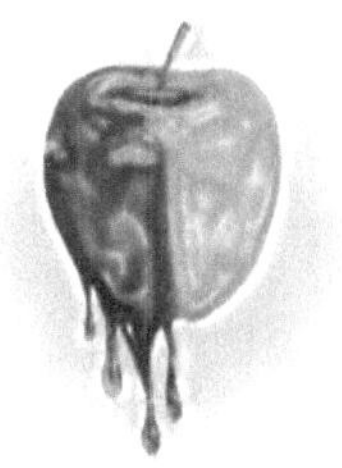

Chapter 18
The Army Returns

We made it back to the castle before Kenshin arrived. Shirayuki promised Ujie that she wouldn't tell anyone that he lost her on guard duty and sent him away with a list of drills to complete in the training room. I suspected she was only being so generous to cover up her own escape.

When Kenshin arrived, Shirayuki bolted for his caravan, leaving me in the dust.

What, you aren't going to greet the heroes coming home? Kagami asked in an innocent voice.

Of course I will, I said.

I slowly made my way through the chaos of the returning soldiers and the servants swarming the area to unload the carts and stable the horses.

Just think, Kagami mused, *if you had ran after*

Shirayuki and used the path she carved before more servants came, you could already be in the warm embrace of any number of those dashing young men.

I ignored her still, steadily making my way through the crowd.

Granted you only care about one of them, don't you?

"Shut up!" I said through gritted teeth.

"But I haven't said anything yet."

I jumped in surprise at Kagekatsu's voice right next to me.

"Oh, not you! I didn't realize you were there, Kagami was just, um..."

"Causing mischief?" he supplied.

"Yes."

"Dad says we won't go out again until the winter season has passed, so you are going to be stuck with me for a while." Kagekatsu nudged me with his elbow.

"Oh no, perhaps now isn't the best time to tell you that I am resigning as resident Itako." I joked.

"Wait, hold on, you can't be serious!"

Kagekatsu gripped my shoulders as if to stop me from fleeing right that moment.

"Of course not!" I said, reaching up and placing my hand on his shoulder. "It's called a joke."

I felt him relax beneath my hand as he took a steadying breath.

"Don't do that to me!" he protested.

Ah, Kagami cooed, *it seems he feels the-*

Shut up! I shouted in my mind. I shook my head as if I could shake Kagami out before smiling at Kagekatsu.

"I'm sorry," I said. "I thought you would know it was a joke. Unfortunately you will be stuck with me until Kenshin decides to go on another conquest."

"Good. I'm quite sick of Kagetora after traveling with him for months. Shirayuki only ever talks about the war, and will be following Kenshin around like she's his shadow. So that just leaves you to entertain me through the long winter months."

I laughed, letting my hand drop from his shoulder. "Well, I'm glad to know I'm your first choice in the company after literally everyone but the staff here."

"Wait no, that's not. Hold on." He lightened his grip on my arms as he struggled for words

I laughed again, gently grabbing his arms to lift his hands off my shoulders, "I was joking Kagekatsu."

He relaxed again, looping my arm through his. "You really need to change your tone of voice or wink or something so I can tell you're joking." he said, chuckling a little bit as he led me back inside the pagoda.

"I don't understand why you don't laugh at my jokes, but everyone else is hilarious to you."

"That's because I can actually tell they're joking, which brings me back to my point. You need a signal to tell people you're joking."

"I really don't think other people have a problem with this." I nudged him with my elbow as we walked.

"See, like that. That was perfect."

"I- wasn't joking..."

Kagekatsu is quiet for a moment. "Seriously?"

"Seriously." I laughed and squeezed his arm as I felt him deflate beside me. "I'm sorry, I almost wish I was joking so you could be right this time."

Kagami nudged me for attention, *Can I speak now?*

I reached down and patted her head with my free hand.

"Yes Kagami, what is it?" I spoke aloud so Kagekatsu didn't think I was ignoring him if I seemed distracted.

"Shirayuki is having a huge fight with Kenshin in the dining hall." Kagami spoke aloud, which meant we must have been alone in this part of the castle.

"That's odd. Usually the first few days Dad is back she tries not to ruffle his feathers by complaining about not being involved in the war more." Kagekatsu said.

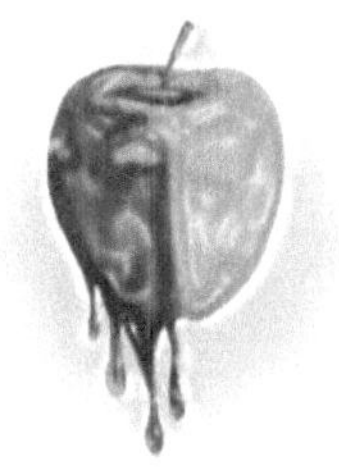

Chapter 19
The Argument

By the time we arrived at the dining hall, their weapons had been drawn.

Over the metallic clang of their swords, Shirayuki would punctuate every strike by shouting insults.

Clang. "How can you call yourself a Samurai if you're weak!"

Clang. "My father believed in you."

Clang. "In your ideals."

Clang. "And you will just throw it all away."

A sword clattered to the ground. "And for what? Your saké?"

"Shirayuki." Kenshin's voice was raw and more ragged than usual. "I understand your concern, but what you're suggesting isn't..."

"Isn't what? It isn't in align with your morals, but drinking your life away and abandoning your children is?"

"Ah, that's what this is about," Kagekatsu whispered in my ear.

"Shirayuki," Kenshin tried again. "You know that's not my intent, but I-"

"Save it for your saké!" Shirayuki shouted and stomped across the dining hall. When she reached us, she shoved past Kagekatsu and muttered, "Thanks for the back-up brother."

"What was that about?" I asked once Shirayuki's footsteps had faded away.

"We don't like to mention it, but dad's health isn't what it once was." Kagekatsu admitted.

"What do you mean?" I asked, shocked at this revelation. Kenshin always seemed so strong and sturdy.

"It's nothing I can't handle." Kenshin grumbled.

"He has gotten worse since we were here last, he has lost weight, isn't eating much, complains of stomach cramps, and has developed a cough."

Kagekatsu explained.

As if to illustrate this point Kenshin let out a bout of coughs.

"Has he seen a doctor?" I asked.

"The best doctors in the city have no idea how to help him." Kagekatsu explained. "Shirayuki is convinced that his love of saké is making the problems worse."

"If I'm going to be miserable, then I might as well get some enjoyment out of my life," Kenshin explained. "I'm not going to give up saké just to make myself more miserable."

"I see." I didn't know what else to say.

After a moment of silence, Kenshin spoke, "Now she is trying to cure me with witchcraft spells that require live sacrifices and would make me stronger and immortal."

"Where did she find such a thing?" Kagekatsu asked.

Dread filled me up, making me feel as if I was filled with stone.

Kenshin sighed, "She must have snuck out or slipped away from a guard. It doesn't really matter now, we just have to make sure it doesn't happen again."

"I'll tell Koga to arrange a guard schedule to watch her. She isn't going to like it though." Kagekatsu said.

"I'll tell her, and I'II try and talk to her about witchcraft." A pit grew in my stomach at the thought of confronting her and her wrath of she didn't understand I was trying to look it for her

"Thanks Yumi," Kagekatsu squeezed my arm before letting me go and walking off to find Koga.

Chapter 20
Shingen

I knocked at Shirayuki's door.

"Go away!" she shouted from the other side.

"Shirayuki," I called. "Please talk to me. Why didn't you tell me that... " I trailed off, not wanting to be overheard.

There was a beat of silence before she responded. "Are you alone?"

"Yes."

The door slid open with a gentle scraping sound just before Shirayuki grabbed my arm and pulled me inside.

"I was going to tell you today about Kenshin's health, but you insisted on bringing Ujie," Shirayuki said after sliding the door closed behind me and Kagami.

"So instead you ran off on your own to do a little shopping?"

"You don't understand! This could save his life!" Shirayuki protested.

If it even works, Kagami scoffed.

I patted her head to let her know I heard her.

"How are you sure this will even work?" I asked.

"Come on Yumi! I thought you of all people would understand." Shirayuki shoved a thick leather-bound book into my hands. "The things in this book. The things we could do if we study and practice would be amazing. We could have an undying army!"

I took a step back. "Is this about Kenshin? Or the war?"

"Both!" Shirayuki gripped my arms. "With this we could save Kenshin and win the war."

"We?" I asked.

"Yes!" Shirayuki's grip tightened. "You are a powerful Shaman. I'll need your help with the spells."

"Spells? Shirayuki, I don't know anything about spells."

"You do spells all the time!" she protested.

"I perform rituals to commune with the dead, but it's not magic. I- I can't help with this." I shoved the book back into her chest, getting her to grab it and let go of me.

I turned away just to come face to face with Takeda Shingen. The Tiger of Kai. Shirayuki's father.

His face was grief stricken as he looked over my head at Shirayuki. I reached out and touched him. He tore his gaze from his daughter and looked at me with pleading eyes. I nodded and his form shimmered as he bent into me and I opened my mind to him.

A cold shiver ran through my body. I turned back to Shirayuki. When I opened my mouth, it was the rich commanding voice of Shingen that came out.

"Shirayuki," I/Shingen said. "Don't do this, don't corrupt yourself with dark magic. There is no honor in selling your soul for power."

There was a long pause before Shirayuki finally spoke. The realization that this was her dead father's voice speaking to her was evident in her voice.

"Of course you would say that. You want Kenshin to die and abandon me, just like you did. All that matters is that you could see him again."

"Shirayuki, I wish with all my heart that I could still be alive and be there for you."

"And Kenshin," Shirayuki interjected.

My head shook of its own accord. "For you, Shirayuki. But my time came, and I met my end with honor in the field of battle. I want you to know that thus far, you have brought honor to the Shingen family. And the Uesugi name as well. Don't stray from your path by experimenting with dark magic and conspiring with witches all for the sake of cheating death and gaining power."

I could hear Shirayuki's breath as it quickened with her raging temper.

"You left me! Abandoned me to a dying man who would ultimately abandon me too. Leaving me with nothing but my tessen and a war to win in your name! You don't get to come here and possess my friend just to judge me! NOW GET OUT!"

"Shirayuki I - "

"Yumi, I mean it, make him leave and tell him

never to come back."

I tried to open my mouth but Shingen was grinding my teeth and I couldn't pry them apart.

"Yumi," Shirayuki warned. "I mean it, I want him gone!"

Finally, Shingen released his hold on me and I fell forward into Shirayuki as his cold presence left my body.

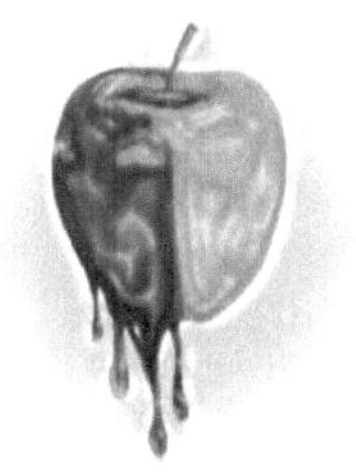

Chapter 21
Outed

Shirayuki held me as we both recovered from the ordeal. We were both shaking, me from the cold, and her from anger. Finally, when warmth had returned to my limbs and I was able to stand on my own, I pulled away from her and held her at arm's length.

"Shirayuki, I'm sorry. He was here, and looked so concerned. I thought hearing from him would help, but I didn't realize it would cause you such distress."

Shirayuki took a deep breath before responding, "Is he usually hanging around me?" her voice was ragged, and I wondered briefly if she could have been crying.

"Sometimes. He likes to watch you train and see how you lead the troops you are training."

"Do you talk with him about me?"

"No" I lied, shaking my head.

"Don't lie to me Yumi."

"I have," I confessed, "Kenshin found me seeking advice from him about you, I obliged, as it was my job."

"That's why he brought you here, you were his link to my dad."

"He also thought you needed a friend. He thought we would get along." I confessed.

"You've been spying on me for him?" She stepped back, shoving me into a chair.

"NO!" I protested. "It's not like that!"

"Oh, and what is it like?"

"He asked me to be the resident Itako, and while I was here to try to be your friend. But I don't report to him. If anything, he asks, and I assure him that you are doing well and are happy aside from the fact that he doesn't include you in the war effort more, but he knows that already. I wouldn't betray your trust. You're my first real friend, if you don't count Kagami."

"So, Kenshin didn't send you up here to try and talk me out of using witchcraft?"

"He sent me here to tell you that he is setting up a new guard schedule to watch you. I'm the one who is worried about how long you have been sneaking out and talking with witches. He doesn't know that you slipped your guard today," I assured her, "but he knows you must have at some point to obtain such a book."

"What new guard schedule?"

"Kenshin wants you watched at all times. You will have a guard posted outside your door. You are still allowed to leave, but you are to be watched at all times."

A soft thud followed by a muffled scream let me know she was not taking the news well.

When she was done she said, "You should go, I'll see you at dinner, I just need to process."

"Of course." I headed to the door.

"Yumi?"

"Yes?"

"Could Kagami stay?"

I bent down and opened my arms and Kagami filled them with her soft form.

Don't show her what you are capable of.

I'm not an idiot Yumi, I know she wouldn't be able to resist having a Kitsune at her side in the field of battle. I have no interest in being dragged into a human war.

Don't let her experiment on you either.

Yumi, seriously, have a little faith!

Just be safe okay?

Always am.

"Yes, she will stay with you as long as you need." I straightened and turned back to the door.

"She isn't going to be my guard right?" Worry and maybe a little paranoia crept into her voice.

"Don't be silly. She is just a pet. I just told her to play nice and not get into any trouble or scratch your furniture."

Shirayuki gave an uneasy laugh, "Right, of course, see you later."

When I reached the door I paused. "Shirayuki?"

"Yes."

"I won't abandon you. You know that right? Your family is bigger than your father and Kenshin."

"Thanks." her voice was small and quiet. I prayed that she believed what I said as I slid the door closed behind me.

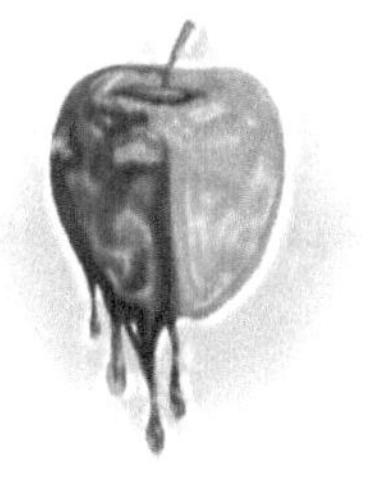

Chapter 22
The Death Poem

As the winter months came and the daylight got scarce, Shirayuki used the cover of night to leave the castle grounds without anyone noticing. Kagami often alerted me of her flight and I would flag down a guard and tell them to begin a search. The first few times I met quite a bit of resistance, but luckily Kagekatsu was usually nearby to convince them that it didn't hurt to check. After being right every time, Koga made sure that all the guards were instructed to listen when I brought up a concern about Shirayuki.

Eventually, she stopped trying to leave without an escort as often. Instead she poured her efforts into caring for Kenshin as his condition worsened. He was constantly clearing his throat and coughing. His voice was getting even more ragged than before. He had lost a lot of weight, and he only seemed to have an appetite for saké, though he was able to handle small meals. With these worsening symptoms, Shirayuki became very protective of him.

Kenshin still insisted on sparing with the rest of his guards everyday despite her protests. She would watch and participate, but as soon as he would grunt in pain or lean on the wall for support, she would insist he sit for the remainder of training. Of course he refused and she would storm off and lock herself in her room for the rest of the day, only answering to me and Kagetora, who always sided with her when the family argued.

It was about halfway into the winter months when Kenshin announced that in the spring he would march on his greatest rival, the only one standing in his way to unite all of Nihon under one shogunate[18]: Nobunaga.

The war preparations began and Shirayuki was only ever either at Kenshin's side advising him or sulking in her room. After two months of this, I was walking past Shirayuki's room when I heard her shout in anger and throw something across the room. I stopped and softly knocked on the door.

---

[18] **Shogunate** /sho-**gun**-ate/ a form of government in feudal Japan, in which power was held by the Shogun, a military dictator.

"Shirayuki," I called. "Are you okay?"

The door slid open with a bang.

"He wrote a flipping death poem Yumi! A DEATH POEM!" A rustle of papers rattled close to my face and I assumed she was waving the death poem itself around.

All I could think to say was, "Huh, a poem? I knew he liked to read but I didn't fancy him a poet."

"That's all you have to say?" Shirayuki shouted, stomping her way into her room.

I stepped inside and slid the door closed behind me.

"I know you care for him, he is like family to you! You should be mad too!" Shirayuki protested my subpar response to her distress.

"I don't see how him writing poetry is really something to be mad about."

"Ugh! It's not just the poetry Yumi! You've seen him. He is wasting away, his armor barely fits him, it's so big; he knows he is dying, that's why he wants to attack Nobunaga as soon as the weather permits! He is hoping to die in battle or win the battle before this sickness takes him!"

"I didn't realize he had lost so much weight," I said. Nobody was ever that descriptive when they told me about it, just that he had.

"You didn't-" she cut herself off. "Oh yeah, right, never mind."

"So, what's this poem say that's got you all worked up." I asked.

Shirayuki lets out an exasperated sigh; it's not just a poem. Poems are fine, I love poems, but this is a DEATH poem. He is admitting defeat. It goes against everything he taught, everything a samurai stands for."

She thrust the poem into my hands. I held them up after a moment.

"Yeah, you're going to need to read it to me." I said.

She snatched the paper out of my hand and groaned.

Even a life-long prosperity

Is but one cup of saké

A life of forty-nine years is passed in a dream

I know not what life is, nor death

Year in year out all but a dream

Both heaven and hell left behind

I stand in the moonlit dawn

Free from clouds of attachment[19]

I sat there silently for a moment.

"That sure is a death poem." I finally said.

"Ugh, you're no help, go away."

"Shirayuki, I don't know what to tell you. I don't think anything you say to him will change his mind about...well, anything really."

"I know," she said quietly. "Honestly I think he is past the point of healing that medical herbs could provide. It's just a matter of time," she heaved a heavy sigh and sniffed, "I just wish it wasn't happening at all." Her voice was strained, and I realized she was crying.

I reached out and gently placed my hand on her shoulder. "I know. I'm sorry."

She threw her arms around me, letting herself give way to body shaking sobs as I held her. "I don't want to lose another father," she whispered into my hair.

---

[19] Death poem reference: (Suzuki, Daisetsu Teitaro (1993) Zen and Japanese Culture. Princeton. Isbn 9780691017709)

That was one of the rare times I heard her call Kenshin father, not uncle. But it was true all the same. He raised her these past five years since Shingen's death. He loved her as a father would.

"I know," I rubbed her back, "I know you don't."

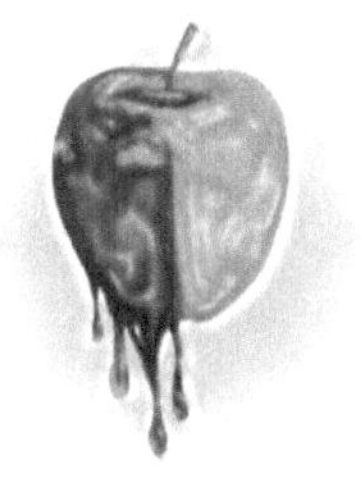

Chapter 23
Broken

It was just over a month later when Kenshin was found dead in the bathroom.

Blood coated the inside of his mouth and there were spots of it on his hand. This wasn't surprising; he had been coughing up flecks of blood for a few weeks now. When Shirayuki saw his body being carried down the halls by the guards, she screamed. The sound echoed through the halls and made my blood fill with dread. When I found her, she was still in the spot where she had seen him, but she had crumpled to the floor. Sobs racked through her body. I knelt beside her and placed my hand gently on her knee. I didn't speak. I just let her know I was there.

After Kenshin's body had been placed in the training room where it would stay until the funeral,

Kagetora came and wrapped his arms around her as she cried herself dry. A little while later, Kagekatsu came and sat with us, leaning on my shoulder as his tears wet my kimono.

***

Finally, finally, Shirayuki quieted enough to speak.

"Why? Why did he have to die!? I was so close, so close to a cure, and he dies before I even had a chance to-" another bout of sobs racked through her and she collapsed onto my lap.

I don't know how long we sat there, Kagekatsu leaning on me, Shirayuki on my lap and Kagetora leaning on Shirayuki, a broken family. But I do know that my mind was filled with questions.

Kagami, I called. She was off tormenting the guards, I'm sure. *I need you to find out what Shirayuki was looking into. What cure she found.*

Are you saying I'm allowed to snoop in her private quarters while she is grieving the death of the man that was like a father to her?

I winced. *You don't have to say it like that... just do it, okay? I thought she told me he was beyond the help of healers. I'm worried she turned again towards more twisted solutions.*

***

When Shirayuki finally stopped crying enough to move, we helped her to her room and had the kitchen staff bring up her favorite meal. I told the guard at her door to come get me or her brothers if she needed anything at all, no matter what time it was. Then I dragged myself back to my own suite and cried myself to sleep.

I'm not usually affected by death, and even though I didn't know Kenshin for very long, barely under a year, he was a good man, who was always kind. And now he was gone, and my heart felt like it was breaking to pieces just like the family he left behind.

My head ached, and my sheets were wet with tears, the fabric sticking to my face when sleep finally overtook me and I embraced the dreamless void of unawareness.

Chapter 24
Vanished

Yumi! Wake up, something has happened.

"Ugh, I know Kagami," I mumbled, groping around for a pillow and pressing it over my face to block the sunlight streaming through the cracks of the window shutters.

No, it's Shirayuki, she's gone.

I sat bolt upright. The sudden movement made me dizzy and I had to steady myself before I could stand.

"What?" I yelled.

I tried to follow her, but after she was in the woods for a while she, I don't know, she became shielded from me. I've been trying to wake you for hours!

Hours? She had been gone for hours?

"I need to speak with the guards." I said rushing to the door and stubbing my toe on the door frame in my haste. I doubled over in pain but still stumbled out to the hallway yelling,

"GUARDS! GUARDS!" I kept yelling as I ran, trailing my hand along the wall heading to the courtyard. Soon enough, a firm hand gripped my elbow accompanied by the voice of a guard I recognized as familiar, but couldn't place at the moment.

"Miss Yumi, I'm here, what is wrong?"

"Shirayuki, where is she?"

"I would assume she is still in her locked room grieving."

"We need to check on her now."

The guards were used to this by now. They didn't question me anymore.

Soon we were at her door. The guard stationed there unlocked it after she didn't answer and searched her room. Then the castle was searched. Once every room had been scoured, the guards began their search of the surrounding area.

Dread filled up my whole being. She had almost

a full day to disappear by the time the guards finally started searching outside the grounds. I let them search the castle first as that's what they insisted would be the best course of action, but I knew she was gone. And every moment she was gone something could happen to her.

***

The search lasted a full week. They searched the town multiple times and began to comb the forest that lay just north of us. The first few days were torture. I was sick with worry. I wouldn't eat and I could barely sleep. But as the guilt dug in, it implanted the unnerving worst case scenario into my head and I couldn't shake it. I couldn't help but let the negative thought fill me with the certainty that I had lost Kenshin's daughter, and she was dead.

Kagekatsu and Kagetora were tireless in their search. They didn't allow a funeral for Kenshin until Shirayuki was home safe. They refused to cease the search after days of nothing.

I became desperate to find her as well. Kagami searched for her soul, her very essence, but couldn't find it anywhere. Strangely enough, she couldn't find it in the spirit realm either. That gave me hope. She wasn't dead if Kagami couldn't find her after scouring the souls of the dead. She was out there somewhere. But for some reason Kagami couldn't find her. It's almost like she didn't want to be found by Kagami, which was worrisome, as I never told her that she was a kitsune.

But if Shirayuki actually managed to shield herself from a kitsune, a seven tailed kitsune no less, that was not something she had done by accident. She had been planning this. My thought spiral ended abruptly and I turned my thoughts toward Kagami.

Kagami!

A slight pressure rested on my knee and I laid my hand on her head before holding her face in both my hands and attempting to stare her down.

Why didn't you tell me what you found when you went snooping in Shirayuki's room?

Because you have been sending me everywhere searching for her in a panic that I didn't think that was the top priority on your mind at the moment. She said innocently but I felt her lips curl up into a smile. She liked the panic and uncertainty floating around. She could feed on it. The emotions were freely thrown about so I couldn't blame her. But she was withholding information to add to it, and I was not happy with her.

"Tell me Kagami!" I shouted.

She winced under my grip. *Okay, okay, so I looked through that spell book and it detailed some pretty wicked black magic that I'd never even heard of. What of it? You already knew that.*

"What spell was she trying to do?" I pressed.

Kagami sighed, *There were a ton of notes scribbled around one in particular...*

"Go on..."

It promised limitless strength and a thirst for blood. It promised that you would be faster than anything and no sickness could befall you. And... it promised immortality.

"That's the cure." I said. "She figured out how to perform the spell. She wanted to do it to Kenshin once she was certain of how to do it, but he...he died before she ever had the chance." I dropped Kagami's head unceremoniously in my lap. "Do you know if she could have done it to herself? Do you think that's what she did? So she could succeed him and fight Nobunaga, fulfill both of her fathers' dreams?"

Kagami sighed and I felt her paw rub her snout before placing it back on the ground. *Yes. This spell, the cost of it, is that you lose your soul. I think that's why I can't find her.*

I sighed and collapsed in a heap on the floor, losing all sense of posture.

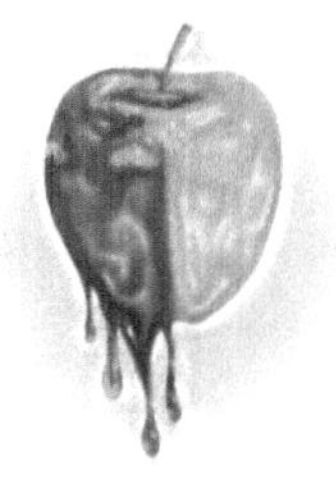

Chapter 25
Found, But Still Gone

The next day I heard shouts from a guard and I hurried to the courtyard, Kagami trailing behind me.

He was out of breath when his thundering footsteps stumbled to a halt. "We found her!" He gasped. "In the woods... so much blood. We have to... we need to get a cot and the doctor immediately."

Kagami go. I need to know. I urged her in my mind and Kagami brushed past me and ran out of the compound to see what the guards had found.

To the guard I said, "Rest. I'll fetch the doctor. And thank you." Tears sprang to my eyes as I ran to find the doctor.

I had just finished helping the doctor ready his

sick bed when there was a commotion outside in the courtyard. I hurried out of the small room and stood aside, pressed against the wall to allow room as the mass of guards' footsteps passed me, escorting Shirayuki's unconscious form into the doctor's room.

While they were getting settled, Kagami pressed her nose to my hand and I saw a flash of images in my mind.

I had been told what Shirayuki looked like on many occasions. She was the epitome of beauty. Her hair was black as ebony, and shined in the sunlight, her eyes were similar to her father's, a haunting brown, her complexion was very fair, almost to the point where she would not need any makeup to make her look any paler, and her lips were full and a healthy dark pink. But the image that Kagami showed me of her rescue chilled me to the bone.

Shirayuki being carried by the guards, her small frail frame was dressed in a ragged night dress. She was covered in dirt and grime from being in the woods and her dark ebony hair was a mess of tangles as leaves and branches stuck out of it. She was covered in blood. Her skin was pale, I knew she was very fair, that's how she got her name; but this, she looked like all the life blood was drained from her body. The only color was her blood stained lips. But the most disturbing change was when she opened her eyes: they were as black as her hair. Two soulless voids watching. Waiting.

I blinked the images away and tears formed in my eyes, "What has she done to herself," I whispered.

It's not her. It looks like her, it smells like her, but it's not her. Her soul, her essence, is different, twisted. Even her mind is different. Beware Yumi, that is not the Shirayuki that you have come to know and care for, that is something different entirely. Kagami's words echoed in my mind.

The guards came out and Kagekatsu and Kagetora pulled me aside to let me know what they knew.

"The doctor is checking in on her now, but she lost so much blood. I know when she was conscious, she was mumbling about blood and how hungry she was, but her pulse is so faint. If she wasn't semi conscious I would have thought she didn't have one. We found her close to the forest's edge, collapsed in a heap. I think she was trying to find her way back to town." Kagekatsu's voice was thick, as though he had been crying.

I nodded, "I'm so glad you found her." I reached for his hand and gave it a squeeze.

"I only hope we weren't too late. First dad and now this," he heaved a weary sigh.

I bit my lip, not knowing what to say.

"I'm going to rest. Come find me if her condition worsens," Kagetora said before shuffling away.

Kagekatsu called after him, "In the morning we will start planning for the funeral rites for dad now that Shirayuki is back home."

"You should rest too, you must be exhausted. I'll wake you with any news." I urged Kagekatsu.

"No, I'll stay a while longer," Kagekatsu said. "I don't want to be alone right now."

Warmth blossomed in my chest at his words. We settled down on the floor outside Shirayuki's sick room and waited in comfortable silence for the doctor to emerge.

It was not long after that when the doctor opened the door and ushered us inside.

"It's the strangest thing," he whispered in a low tone to not be overheard. "There isn't a scratch on her. Not even a bruise, she is flawless."

"That's not possible. She was stumbling about the forest for a week. Surely there is at least one scratch. Not to mention she was caked with blood. Where did that come from?" Kagekatsu argued.

"Not a scratch. See for yourself."

Kagekatsu let go of my hand so he could kneel and examine her body.

"But, she was covered in blood." I said.

"Yes, I don't think it was hers. I had a servant come and bathe her once I was sure there were no wounds for me to treat so I could see if I'd missed some superficial wounds under all that blood and grime. She was flawless, not a scratch," his voice took on a wistful tone, "she sure is a lucky girl, and so beautiful..."

I held in my disgusted scoff.

Finally, the doctor came back to himself. "She is quite cold to the touch though, I've ordered some more blankets to her room and I'll have her moved up there shortly."

I nodded and thanked the doctor before Kagekatsu and I left. I told him to rest, then set off to Shirayuki's quarters. The servants were just leaving the blankets and I asked one to get a chair for me outside her room. Then two guards stomped down the hallway and placed her sleeping form on her bedroll. The servants busied themselves tucking the extra blankets around her and the guards took up their post by the door next to my seat.

"I'll watch for her out here," I told them sitting down in my chair. "You should stand guard outside her window.

"With all due respect Miss Yumi, I think at least one of us should stand guard here as well." One of the guards said cautiously.

"Don't worry, my Kagami will help me keep an eye out, nothing will be missed. You can have a guard resume their post here after she has woken up and I've spoken with her."

At the mention of Kagami, her head nuzzled under my arm and rested on my lap.

The guards left me in peace after that.

I had considered waiting in her room, but Kagami's warning still ran fresh in my ears, *She is not the Shirayuki you knew.*

I sat there the rest of the day and through the night. Kagami kept me company. We played a rousing game of guess who likes who in the castle staff. When it was time for the guards to do a shift change, they asked to take over, but I insisted I was fine. I didn't want a guard to be the first person she saw when she woke up.

In the morning, I finally heard her stir. I waited a few minutes before I knocked softly on her door.

"Shirayuki?" I asked softly. "Would you like me to have someone bring you up some breakfast?"

"No." Her voice was barely a whisper.

"Would you like me to stay close?" I asked.

I heard the padding of her feet and the door slid open slightly. "Were you out there all night?" she asked.

"I was worried about you," I said.

"You look awful."

"I'm sure I do," I said with a laugh.

"Terrible bags under your eyes," she sighed. "Come in."

I waited. She didn't move. I knew that she had only slid the door open a crack and was peeking her head out. I hadn't heard the door open any farther. I realized she was trying to get me to walk into the door, but I was so used to Kagami's antics that a little trick like this wouldn't fool me. I smiled and waited patiently.

We stood like that for a long time, silent, until finally she sighed, and I heard her faint footsteps as she pushed the door open and walked back towards her bedroll. I stepped inside her room and a chill shivered up my spine.

"You know, if you didn't want me to come in, you could have just said so," I said, trying to ease the tension in the room. I walked along the far wall before leaning against it.

"I know," she said.

"How are you feeling?" I asked.

"I feel fine. Better than fine. I feel great," she said. Her voice did not sound like a starved girl who spent a week in the woods scavenging for food.

"Are you cold? Do you need any more blankets? Or perhaps someone could light your fire?"

"No, I'm perfectly comfortable."

I frowned. She was usually pretty particular about her fire being kept burning at all times, complaining that her feet were cold. From the feel of how cold her room was, I'd say the fire burnt out sometime yesterday afternoon and she was without heat all night. But instead of bringing this up, I just shrugged.

"Okay," I gestured to the window. "You climbed out your window then? Scaled three flights down to the gardens below? We'll have guards posted outside your room and below your window so you won't have to look far for an escort next time you wish to take a late night stroll."

"Ugh, you're insufferable."

I heard her stomp her foot on the ground. At the same time I felt a strong vibration in the floor. Fear flickered over me. I was so tired, tired of being worried, tired from staying up all night. I just wanted answers and she was playing games.

"I feel like that's quite reasonable actually. I can understand why you ran away. And that you didn't want an escort watching your every move, especially after seeing Kenshin's dead body being carried away. But you were gone for a week. We thought the worst, and they found you covered in blood, barely conscious. You can understand why your brothers want extra protection around you. Right?"

She scoffed.

She rolled her eyes at you, Kagami told me.

My patience snapped. I wanted to understand her and for her to understand that we weren't trying to lock her away, just keep her safe. But I wasn't getting anywhere with her. She shut me out.

"No? You don't think so? Let's try it this way.

The night your father died you ran away, had your brothers worried sick, and all the guards looking for you for a full week. All the while you went out to play with black magic. I could ask to have you locked up for messing with forces you don't understand, potentially endangering the townsfolk. Where did all that blood come from Shirayuki? What or who did you kill when you were out there?"

Something shifted in the air. I felt a cold evil presence begin to permeate the room. Shirayuki groaned in frustration.

Kagami curled her tail around my feet. *There she is. She can't bury it for long. Times up and now we can see her for what she has become.*

I only vaguely understood what Kagami was talking about. But I figured if I wanted answers she would be the most vulnerable now.

"What have you done to yourself, Shirayuki?" I shouted.

Shirayuki's laugh was cold and calculating.

There's a dark void where her soul should be, Kagami whispered, her tail shook as she tried to hold back any reaction she had to Shirayuki.

"I did what Kenshin couldn't bring himself to do. Oh, I tried. For years I tried to convince him to let me join the fight so that we could be the immortal rulers of Nihon, and soon the world. But he never listened. Even when he was on death's door he laid down and accepted defeat. Even when I offered him strength far greater than anyone could imagine and youthful vitality for years to come. But you know what he said to me? Every time he told me to stop messing with forces I didn't understand. He treated me like a *child*. He never let me on the battlefield, he never let me lead because he was scared that the little girl he loved so much would turn into a bloodthirsty monster. He told me I could never become the ultimate warrior and forbade me from ever trying it," she laughed. Another chill ran down my spine. "But now? Dear old uncle Kenshin is dead. He can't tell me what to do anymore," she sang.

I stumbled backwards into the corner. Tripping over Kagami who squeezed out between me and the wall placing herself between me and Shirayuki, growling.

"You didn't... you couldn't have."

"Kill him? No, no, I loved him too much. I let nature run its course, still holding out hope that he would come to his senses and finally listen to me."

A sigh of relief passed over me and I almost collapsed to the floor.

"Surely you knew the price for this power you've gained. Shirayuki, your soul... It's gone," I whispered, clutching at my aching heart. "A black void rests in your center. I don't know what you are anymore."

Shirayuki scoffed, "Who needs a soul? That's what makes you weak. If I'd lost mine years ago I would've had the strength to do what needed to be done and not waited around for Kenshin to finally let me lead."

"No, you can't," I gasped. "I won't let you. I won't let you lead the army. I won't let you turn them into that." I gestured toward her in disgust.

"Who is going to stop me, you?" she spat.

"Yes." I closed my eyes, spread my hands, and began chanting. My hair that had long since escaped my bun lifted from my shoulders. Power surged through me as Kagami lent me her strength. Wind tore through the room, opening her shutters and letting the morning sun stream through them. Shirayuki hissed and tried to block the sun from her eyes. I couldn't see her, but in this state I could feel her movements through the rushing wind along with everything else in the room. A blanket got swept up and wrapped around her tightly and another and another. Until she was wrapped up like a roll of sushi. I chanted and called the wind as I moved towards the exit. Finally when my back bumped against the door, I spun her onto her bed and quickly opened the door, rushing out and sliding it shut behind me. Panting and gasping for air, my fingers gripped the edge of the door and frame tightly to prevent her from opening it. Even though I was sure she could tear it down without much of a struggle.

Guards rushed towards me at the sound of the commotion.

"Don't." I said when they tried to walk in the room to check on Shirayuki. "She's possessed. She needs to be in isolation until I can rid her of the demon."

You know that's not possible. I don't know much about the dark magic that turned her into this but, I don't think it's reversible.

"I'll find a way," I said through gritted teeth. "I'll find a way to get her back."

Chapter 26
A Mystery

I paced my room, trying to think of what rituals I could perform to cleanse Shriayuki's soul of its blackness. I was coming up blank. She wasn't possessed like I had said, there was no demon residing in her. It's like she had turned herself into one. And no cleansing ritual I knew could change a demon back to their original form. If that was even what she was.

Kagami pressed her head against my hand and I felt her warm presence envelop me.

"What do we know?" I asked. I had sent her to watch Shirayuki and try to read her mind to figure out what's happening.

I didn't want to mention this earlier because I wanted to go back and be absolutely certain, but... I don't think she is breathing.

"Kagami of course she is breathing, she is walking around talking. She has to be breathing."

Except she isn't. There isn't a breath left in her being... I... I'm not even sure her heart is beating.

"How can this be?"

I don't know, but that combined with the fact that her soul is gone makes me think of necromancy, but this is different. Twisted, even by necromancy standards.

I shuddered. Necromancers could reanimate the dead. Master Fujmori was one but I never witnessed him perform any magic. But when they reanimated the bodies, their souls were bound to the will of the necromancer; they were essentially puppets. But Shriayuki's mind was all her own. But now lacked any empathy and seemed to have gained strength beyond what was humanly capable.

We'd have to move her to a more secure place that could hold up against her abuse if we wanted to keep everyone in the castle safe.

I need to consult with my sisters, Kagami said eventually.

"What? But you said you would never go back there."

Yeah well. Desperate times and all that. Maybe

they have seen something like this before. I'm going to go consult with them.

"You don't have to do that."

I know, but Shirayuki, whatever she is now, it disturbed me. I'm not going to let my personal feelings for my annoying sisters get in the way of figuring this out. I have to at least ask them.

"Okay. Go then. And hurry back."

***

Kagami was gone for a full five days. In those five days we lost four guards to Shirayuki.

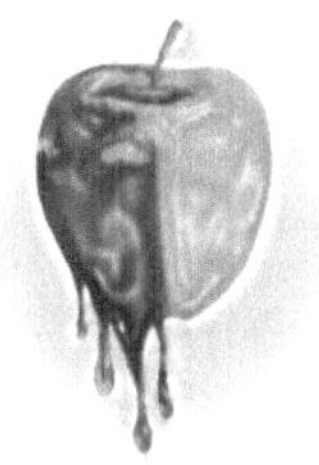

Chapter 27

Assassins on the Loose

The first death of a guard happened two days after Shirayuki's return. She kept to her room and never touched her food. Kagetora was worked up into a ball of nerves fearing she would waste away, but nothing we did could get her to eat. She simply turned up her nose at it and sent it back to the kitchen. Kagekatsu made sure the guards rested and switched shifts often so as to always have them be alert and attentive in case she tried anything.

On the second day, in the dark of the night, one of the guards posted by her window left to check the perimeter of the surrounding garden to ensure there weren't assassins lurking in the bushes. When he returned he found his fellow guard pale as death, drained of all his blood and a bite on his neck. He immediately raised the alarm.

When I arrived, new guards had been posted by Shirayuki's window and the dead were brought to the main hall. Koga directed me, Kagekatsu, and Kagetora to the surviving guard who was on duty in the garden.

The guard, Fujioka Gin, told us what she could. But she was clearly shaken.

"It was the strangest thing," Fujioka said. "There was no blood staining her uniform, not puddled beneath her form, not trickling out of the wound. Nothing."

I agreed that it was odd indeed and Kagekatsu gave Fujioka a few days off to clear her head before she had to report back to duty.

"Wait." I said as the guard's setta started to shuffle away. "What was their name again?"

"Atagi Tsubu."

"Thank you," I said bowing.

"I'll notify her family," Kagetora volunteered.

"Thank you brother," Kagekatsu said as his brother plodded away.

***

The next night the same thing happened. A guard, when left unattended under Shirayuki's window died without any sign of a struggle, or a sound heard from the other guards.

I decided to ask Shirayuki about it the next day.

"Shirayuki?" I called through her door. "May I come in? I'd like to speak with you."

The door opened and I was hit with a blast of cold from her fireless room. I shivered and shoved old memories of my initiation down where they belonged, in the past.

"Would you like me to get someone to start a fire?" I asked, closing the door behind me and wrapping my shawl tighter around my shoulders.

"No, I feel fine," she answered, her voice steady and confident. Considering she was refusing all food from the kitchen, this concerned me.

"Well, as long as you're comfortable," I conceded. "The reason I came is, I don't know if you heard but one of the guards outside your window was killed last night." I strained my ears to hear a reaction from her, but if she looked surprised or did anything, I couldn't see to know, and I didn't hear a gasp.

"This is actually the second guard to die on duty guarding you in the past week... I was wondering if perhaps you heard anything that would help us in the investigation."

"No, I was sleeping soundly in my bed, I didn't hear a thing," she said sweetly. Her voice dripped with honey, and I knew she was lying.

"I feared as much," I confessed. "It is the strangest thing, we don't know who or what could be behind these attacks, and I'm worried for your safety. Would you like to be moved to a different room? It seems these attacks are targeted at those guarding you, so you might be in danger."

"I like my room just fine."

"But-"

"Is that all you wanted?" Shirayuki changed the subject, cutting me off.

"Yes."

"Then I think I'd like to get back to reading now, thank you." I heard the rustle of papers that I assumed were a book and I hesitated, wondering if I should press her more. I decided that if I was going to confront her, I'd need Kagami's strength to defeat her if she decided to get violent, so I simply nodded and left.

Oh Kagami, I thought, *when are you going to come back? I need you.*

Of course there was no reply, she was conversing with her sisters in the spirit realm, and they did not like to be interrupted. She wouldn't come back until she exhausted every source of knowledge they had about our little problem.

Meanwhile, I was left with a mystery assassin killing off guards, and I couldn't shake the feeling that the mystery assassin was much closer to home than I would like.

Chapter 28
Confirming Suspicions

The next night another two guards died. This time I was almost sure of my suspicions, but I didn't dare voice them aloud. Not even to Kagekatsu. I waited for Kagami's return.

It wasn't the window guards this time. Koga had doubled up the guards with instructions for their safety to never go off alone. They would patrol in twos or threes and never leave a man behind at a post. But even that didn't deter the bloodthirsty beast after the guards. This time they struck inside the castle. The guards right outside Shirayuki's room were both drained of their blood.

They were both found slumped against either side of her door when the next shift of guards came to relieve them.

"How did neither of them see the attack

coming?" I asked.

"I don't know, my only guess is that they did not see their attacker as a threat until it was too late." Koga gave a weary sigh. I knew this was hard on him, losing so many men.

"But, how?" Kagetora asked, "For there to be no blood in the body like you say, how did the other not see the first get drained? Wouldn't you think it to be a long process to drain a healthy young man of all his blood?"

"I think that we are dealing with something not of this world, so I am not at liberty to say how long it might take for this, this beast to drain one of my men of their blood." Kagekatsu speculated.

I sighed heavily and reached out, fumbling a bit to find the chair I knew was nearby and sat in it.

"Who are they?" I asked.

"I do not know Miss Yumi, but I can assure you that I will—" I cut Koga off.

"No, the guards, which ones died tonight?"

There was a long pause. Sometimes I think they forget that I am without my sight, I generally can identify everyone of the house staff with the culmination of their gait, and voice, so when I ask about the lifeless prone bodies I know must be in front of me from the smell of death radiating from them, they seem confused that I can't identify them.

"Enya Sadharu and Ujie Yasutoshi"

"Thank you." I stood up and began to walk away.

"Miss Yumi," Koga called after me, stalling my escape. "Is it true you are… " he paused, "well aren't you an Itako?"

"Yes." I said adjusting the bamboo strapped to my back that held my certification papers.

"Then, well, forgive me. I don't know how it works, but it seems to me that you could…" Koga was at a loss for words. Most were when asking me to perform my Itako duties. For many, death is a fearsome thing and they wish to never speak of it, let alone with it.

"I could. I did. With the first two, they had little memory of what happened. Just boring guard duty then a soft thud behind them, but before they could turn to look, pain. And then they grew dizzy and blacked out, soon after that, they were dead. I'm hopeful to learn more with these guards, if they are willing to speak with me."

The hall grew very quiet and nobody had a

response for me.

"Do you have anything else you want to ask?"

"No, Miss Yumi."

I bowed in his direction, and turned towards my chambers.

***

I went to my closet and drew out a small wooden box. In it I knew was everything I needed to call upon the dead. Of course it was easier when Kagami was around, and I didn't always need them when the dead came to me or were eager to speak with the living, like Kenshin's dear friend, Shingen, the father of Shirayuki.

I brought the box over to the middle of my room and sat down, placing it in front of me. I readjusted the strap on my shoulder until the bamboo rested comfortably in its familiar place. Inside the bamboo, along with my Itako papers certifying me to perform my duties as an Itako, it also carried a protective charm that was primarily used to capture animal spirits who try and possess people. I wouldn't be needing it today, but I liked having it on, especially when I was going to perform a ritual.

I opened the small box and reached inside.

Fingering the items, I took out my gehobako[20], a smaller wooden box, and placed it off to the side. I wouldn't need this either. Inside were more protection charms and small figurines that I use in certain rituals, but not today. That left only a few more things inside. My rosary —a long, beaded necklace with animal jaw bones and teeth strung among the beads; I usually was wearing these along with my bamboo, but I didn't stop to put them on when I heard the commotion this morning. I also had pouches that usually were filled with rice and salt, but I'd used them up yesterday. I rubbed the beads and bones in my lap while I waited. Soon enough there was a knock on my door.

"Come in," I called.

I heard the door open and the soft footfalls of a maid servant's bare feet come in.

"You asked for a small box of rice and salt?" she asked. Her voice was unsure and small; this was Urakami Mitsu.

"Yes, Urakami. Thank you, you can just place them here." I moved my now empty wooden box behind me and patted the spot where it had vacated.

---

[20] **Gehobako** /ge-ho-ba-ko/ Small wooden box containing figurines and charms used in shamanic rituals.

"Do you need anything else, Miss Yumi?"

"No thank you. And can you make sure I'm not to be disturbed unless there is an emergency until noon? And that no patrols will venture in this wing?"

"Um, sure."

"You don't need to fear, and it's not the end of the world if people do come this way. It's just an added precaution. I'll be performing the appropriate protection spells, the kami[21] will watch over this house."

"Alright, I'll be sure the rest of the staff knows you are not to be disturbed."

"Thank you."

"And —"

"Yes?"

"Well I just thought perhaps you didn't know, Shirayuki has gained some color to her cheeks today,"

"Has she eaten since—?"

---

[21] **Kami** /kah-mee/ - revered deities and spirits in the shinto religion, interconnected with nature and the natural world.

"No, and no firewood has been used, she keeps her windows drawn shut, there is no light in her room when we bring her meals."

"Thank you for letting me know Urakami, I'll be sure to check on her again later today."

I heard the rustle of her kimono as she bowed and closed the door, leaving me alone.

This new information troubled me, but hopefully I'd get answers to those questions after communing with the dead.

Kuchiyose[22] ceremonies are usually just that: ceremonies. A cultural tradition performed at our funerals. However, I had questions that most mourners wouldn't think to ask. And I believed they held answers that we might not want to broadcast throughout the village, stirring up rumors about the Uesugi household only weeks after his own death, while we were preparing for his funeral. It was supposed to be held last week, but with the guards dying left and right, we thought having a public funeral would be an invitation for an assassin, and we were forced to postpone as we assessed the threat that loomed over our house.

---

[22] **Kuchiyose** /koo-**chee**-yo-seh / - Literally translated to 'drawing in to speak' it refers to the practice of allowing spirits to possess one's body and speak through it.

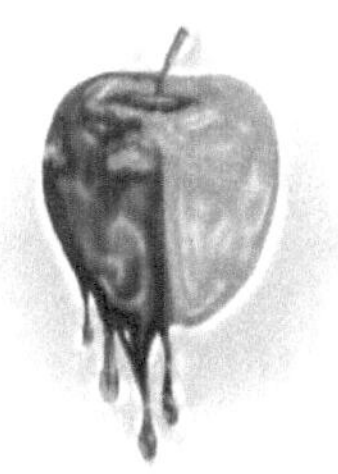

Chapter 29

Communing with the Dead

I began to go through the motions for the ceremony for the guard named Enya Sadaharu. I reached forward and grabbed a handful of rice and a handful of salt in either hand and scattered them around my floor in a big arc. And I began to sing. The kudoki[23], or ritualistic songs, that I sing are old and familiar to me. The words and rhythm feel comforting.

First, I call for the kami to come and protect those in and around my area from being possessed by evil spirits during the ceremony, then I finally get to the calling forth of ghosts. I begin to lose myself in the song as I pour my heart out in the words. I concentrate on Enya and soon I see the flicker of bluish light that tells me a spirit is near. I

---

[23] **Kudoki** /koo-doh-kee/ - Songs used in shamanic and shinto rituals.

continue my song, calling him closer. I need to make sure it is the right spirit before I allow him to enter my mind.

His blurred form takes place in front of me and I can make out the guard's uniform that matched the ghosts of the previous two guards I had summoned not days before. His face is not familiar to me, for I had never seen it before, but his aura was. I pulled him closer and allowed him to enter my mind and body.

The merging of a spirit with an Itako is a strange feeling. It's like taking an ice cold bath while being wrapped in a warm blanket. All of your nerve endings are tingling from the cold but your skin feels warm to the touch. I take a moment to breathe through the discomfort before I speak with him.

"Sir Enya? It is Miss Yumi." I don't usually introduce myself to the dead, but I don't usually know the dead that I am conversing with. "Can you tell me what happened the night you died?" I ask.

Terror grips my soul and I feel my mouth open and close as he tries to use my vocal cords. "She is a monster." He croaks out in my voice.

"Who? Who did this to you?"

"She... she'll be the death of us all."

"Please I must know so we can protect the rest of the guards and the town from her. Show me what happened."

"No. No. Please don't make me go back there."

Tears fell freely down my face.

"I won't make you, but please, I need to know what I'm dealing with." I could feel my heartbeat accelerate as his anxiety gripped him and held him in his terror. "Please!" I cried out gripping my chest in an attempt to stop the pain.

A blinding white light pierced through the blackness of my vision as he thrust me into his memory.

***

It was cold. The hallway by her door always seemed colder since her return, as she never lit a fire anymore to heat it. Enya looked around bored and made a face at Ujie. His companion rolled his eyes and schooled his face back into a serious one. That's when the door to Shirayuki's room slid open. She peeked her head out into the dimly lit hallway. Her face looked timid and perhaps scared.

"I think I saw something in my room, please you must kill it at once," she said.

Enya looked over her head at his companion

and shrugged. "Okay, what did you see?"

"I think it was a rat. It was huge and it scurried right into my bed, I'm sure of it." She cast a worried glance into her room and looked back up at him with pleading eyes.

Enya sighed and followed her into the room. He made his way towards the bed when he heard the door slide close. He turned and looked at her, his eyebrow raised. This was not proper.

"Well, I can't very well have the rat escape." She said with a sneer.

All of her fear seemed to have vanished. But Enya simply shrugged, and turned back to her bed and began to check it for a critter. When he was satisfied that there was nothing there, he turned to leave but Shirayuki was right behind him. Her black soulless eyes gleaming. He jumped back in surprise at her close proximity, and that's when she pounced. She leaped from the ground, launching herself at him and sank her teeth into his neck. Her hand clamped around his mouth so he wouldn't scream. He squirmed and fought against her, but she was stronger than he would have ever imagined. Soon enough, the blood loss was too much for him and he began to feel dizzy. Together, they collapsed onto her bed, Shirayuki's bite never once letting up, and darkness crept in.

***

I gasped for breath when the memory ended. I could still feel Shirayuki's hand over my mouth, smothering me. Her teeth pierced into my neck, my body losing its warmth as she drained my blood. No, not my blood, Enya's. I took many deep breaths to calm my racing heart, but nothing helped. Finally, I spoke to Enya.

"Thank you, I will make sure Shirayuki is dealt with."

The spirit of Enya sighed and I felt him leave my body with another rush of cold pouring inside me, leaving me feeling empty.

I took up my song again. This time concentrating on Ujie. I knew now who the culprit was, I knew that Shirayuki had changed into something unearthly and evil, but I had to still talk to Ujie, just in case he saw or knew anything else that would help me.

Soon enough he appeared in front of me and I invited him in.

The rush of cold still took my breath away, even though I couldn't fathom being any colder. It took me a little longer to catch my breath this time.

"Hello Ujie, it's me, Miss Yumi," I began, "can

you tell me what happened the night you died?"

This time anger ripped through me.

"How could I let this happen!" he roared.

"Ujie, I—"

"If I hadn't been so lax, then this wouldn't have happened and Shirayuki," his voice broke. "Shirayuki would still be—" a sob escaped from me and I wiped the hot tears that were falling freely from my eyes.

I had forgotten, Ujie was smitten with Shirayuki. She liked to lead him on, but ultimately she had no affection for him other than that he would let her get away with breaking some rules. Ujie seemed to blame himself for what Shirayuki has turned into.

"Ujie please, show me what happened I promise I'll do what I can to help her." I said.

***

The blinding white light came again and I was back inside the dimly lit hallway in front of Shirayuki's door. This time I looked over and saw Enya make a face at me/Ujie and I felt him roll his eyes and focus again at the wall ahead. Then Shriayuki's door opened.

"I think I saw something in my room, please you must kill it at once," she said, her gaze focused on Enya, not giving Ujie a second glance. Jealousy stabbed in his heart, but he kept his face neutral and didn't react.

Enya looked over her head at him and shrugged. "Okay, what did you see?"

"I think it was a rat. It was huge and it scurried right into my bed, I'm sure of it." She cast a worried glance into her room and looked back up at Enya with pleading eyes. Ujie's stomach churned at the sight.

Enya sighed and followed her into her room. The door shut softly behind him and Ujie balled his hands into fists and took a steadying breath. It felt like they were in there forever. Ujie strained his ears to hear if they were whispering to each other, but it was deathly silent on the other side of the door, then, was that a grunt? A muffled cry? Ujie was about to barge into the room when he heard a thump of what could only be bodies falling onto the bed.

Anger and jealousy poured into his veins. Blood pounded in his ears. He ran his hands through his hair and began to pace in front of her door. What should he do? He couldn't leave his post. And he definitely didn't want to go in there and see her wrapped up in another man's embrace. He didn't think his heart could take it.

He was about to knock on the door and ask if the rat was found when it opened and Shirayuki's slim figure slipped out, closing it behind her. She looked up at Ujie through her lashes and batted them at him. His mind went blank. He remembered being angry, but she didn't look like she was just locked in an embrace with Enya.

"Ujie, I'm scared. It doesn't seem like Enya will ever find that dreadful rat." She pouted up at him.

"Would you like me to find it for you?" he asked, wanting nothing more than to stay right here in the hallway with her.

"No Enya can look all night if he must. I'd much rather spend my time here with you." Shirayuki reached out and ran her fingers along his sleeve.

Ujie licked his lips. "Is that so?"

"Mmmhmmm."

Suddenly the distance between them closed and Shirayuki had latched herself onto Ujie. A sharp pain was felt in his neck as her teeth sank into his flesh and he let out a soft cry, but Shriayuki's hand across his lips silenced him. For a moment he held her perfectly still in the hallway, not wanting this moment to end, but then his shock wore off and he noticed a few things.

He felt a pull in his neck much deeper than a kiss should offer. He felt his limbs begin to feel cold as blood was sucked out of his body. He thought briefly of the bloodless bodies of his fallen comrades and how the only sign of attack was a single bite mark on the neck.

Panic gripped his heart. But at this point, he was already feeling dizzy and he sank to the floor. Not once did Shirayuki's death grip loosen. She moaned with pleasure as he lay prone on the floor, his blood flowing freely out of him, and then darkness crept into his vision.

***

Another gasp escaped me as I came back to the present. I shivered as the feeling of my blood being pulled and pulled and pulled out of me still lingered in my veins.

"Thank you Sir Ujie."

"You won't kill her, will you?" my voice croaked as he asked.

"I will do everything I can to help her before I

even think about killing her."

I felt him nod my head. "Thank you Miss Yumi."

I sent him away and felt the rush of cold as his soul left my body. I took a steading breath and waited a short while for heat to enter my core before I took up my songs again. These dismissed all spirits who answered my call. And finally I repeated a parting and protection spell three times to ensure all spirits would find their way back to the spirit realm and if any decided to stay they wouldn't be permitted to possess those in this house.

When I was done, I laid on my back on the ground, caught my breath, and calmed my nerves.

"Oh Kagami," I whispered aloud, "where are you when I need you?"

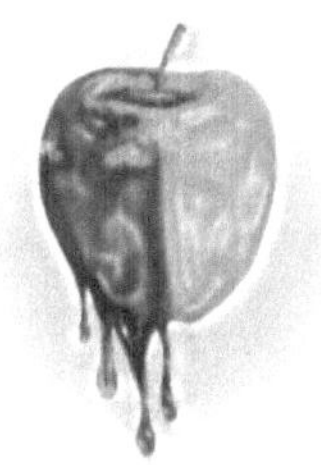

Chapter 30
The Unthinkable Solution

First Kenshin falls ill and dies, then his daughter and my... well, I thought we were friends– turns into a literal bloodthirsty monster. I rubbed my temples as a headache began to pound against my skull. I wiggled the bamboo shaft out from behind me so I wasn't lying directly on it.

I don't know how long I laid there, letting everything that has happened over the past two weeks wash over me, but eventually my stomach growled. I peeled my hands away from my face, now wet with tears. I pushed myself back into a sitting position, and the scattered rice and salt dug into my hands. This would be a huge hassle to clean. I still hated asking maid servants to go clean up my room, even after living here for a little over a year. But I had to admit that I would undoubtedly miss most of the mess and I would have to reclean it for weeks until I got it all. I just had to hope they wouldn't be too upset with having to sweep rice and salt from my floors for a third time in the last week. I placed everything that I had strewn on the floor back inside my wooden box, aside from my rosary. I stood, brushing my hands off on my kimono to get the salt and rice that was sticking to them off, before grabbing my box and placing it in my chest of clothes.

I found my way to the kitchen, made myself a bowl of rice, and grabbed a glass and filled it with water. I sat at a low table off to the side of the kitchen where the staff usually ate. Urakami, the maid servant who brought me the rice and salt came by and asked how it went. I told her it was informative, though I did leave a bit of a mess.

I could hear the smile on her face as she gave a small laugh and said, "I figured you would. After all, this isn't the first time you have performed rituals in your room."

"I know, I just feel bad for making such a mess and not cleaning it up."

"It's fine, and really no trouble. Your room is always so clean, we hardly ever need to do anything in there. And it is a breeze to sweep your uncluttered floors.

I allowed a small smile; I enjoyed hanging out with the other staff.

"When I was still training to be an Itako, sweeping was one of my household duties. It really helped me gain my spatial awareness, but I hated the chore. No matter what I did I always missed a crumb, and I felt like it was impossible to pick up the pile at the end." I thoughtfully twirled my chopsticks in my hand.

"I've always said it is impossible to get a perfect sweep. There is just no way to get it all, and I can see-" Uakami's voice stopped short as she realized that she brought attention to my disability.

"It's fine" I reached out my hand and she grasped it. "I am not so blind that I don't know it."

She snorted in an attempt to hold in her laughter.

"Oh come on," I said, "that was funny! I deserve more than poorly masked laughter."

She gave me a good laugh, and when I joined her she seemed to relax.

"Seriously though, I wish people didn't tiptoe around the fact that I'm blind. I know it. You know it. You can say it. And we can all move on with the conversation without me having to let you know that it's okay and validate your feelings about my feelings that weren't even bothered in the first place. It's all just too complicated. "

The maid servant was quiet for a bit and I felt like perhaps I was too blunt. Oh well. Hopefully Kagami will be back soon so I'll have someone that I can be myself around.

"Well it's getting late, I should probably get to cleaning your floor and finish my other chores so I can do my nightly rounds before it gets dark," Urakami says.

I sighed deeply and bid her farewell.

I finished my rice in silence as the kitchen workers bustled around me. Everything felt disconnected and disjointed, as though maybe these past few weeks have been a dream. Or perhaps I've left my body and I'm observing as someone else lives my life as me. The pounding in my head doesn't help, of course.

The sound of someone sitting across from me brings me out of my thought spiral. I lift my head out of my hand and look in their general direction.

"Miss Yumi," the gentle voice of Kagekatsu made my heart pound as much as my head. "Are you feeling okay?"

"It's Shirayuki." I say quietly, almost inaudible.

He was quiet for a long time, I began to fear that he might not have heard me. And I didn't want to repeat myself louder and have the kitchen staff overhear and cause a panic.

"I feared as much." He finally responds. "I wonder why she hasn't left this place, it certainly would be easier for her if she didn't need to sneak around."

I cocked my head to the side, "I thought that was obvious. She wants to succeed her father as daimyō. She is probably just biding her time until after the funeral so she can challenge you and Kagetora and rightfully take over the clan. Then, since she also has a claim to the Takeda clan she will challenge her older brother who took Shingen's place. With 2 of the main clans united and their armies combined under her control, not to mention her new found strength, it would be fairly simple to take on Nobunaga. Then she would have all of Nihon united under her rule. Just like Kenshin and Shingen always wanted to do."

There was a long silence before anyone spoke.

"She told you this?" Kagekatsu asked.

"Well no. But, it's kind of been her whole goal since she was a kid. It's why she wanted to be a part of the war effort and trained so hard. She wanted to be strong enough to succeed her fathers."

"Well, it would be disastrous if she became the daimyō." Kagekatsu said.

"I know, and I don't know what to do to stop it," I groaned and buried my face in my hands. Very unladylike, for certain, but I stopped caring about appearances over the years.

"I know that you don't want to hear this, but I think we need to consider a more, uh, permanent solution to Shirayuki's.... episodes." This was Koga, the captain of the guard. He spoke softly; I could just hear him over the bustle of the kitchen dishes being washed in the sink clinking and sloshing around. He must have come with Kagekatsu.

Panic gripped my heart at his words, "I can't give up on her just yet. We might still be able to help her. I've sent for more information and help from powerful shamans, perhaps they have seen this before..." It was a long shot, but I was not ready to admit she was beyond my help.

"I agree with Yumi," Kagekatsu said. "We can't give up on her, she is family. In the meantime, we double down on her restrictions. We move her to the top of the tower. Bar the windows, and reinforce the locks on the doors. No one is allowed to see her under any circumstances. Only one of us or Kagetora will bring her meals once a day, she doesn't eat them anyways but if she starts, then we can increase the amount when we come to that. We still guard the door, but the guards are to be under strict order to never open the doors to her chambers, even if she seems distressed, they are to report to you, me or Kagetora first."

"I do not wish to see any harm come to her either. This seems to be the best option for now, but if Miss Yumi is unable to cure her..." Koga's voice trailed off.

"I don't even want to think about it, but yes if it comes to that, we will have to kill her before she devours the entire town." Kagekatsu admitted.

My heart hurt as guilt wracked through me. Tears burned in my eyes. All I could think of was that promise I made to her not too long ago, that I would never abandon her. And now, if I couldn't help her, I was ashamed that I agreed that she would need to die.

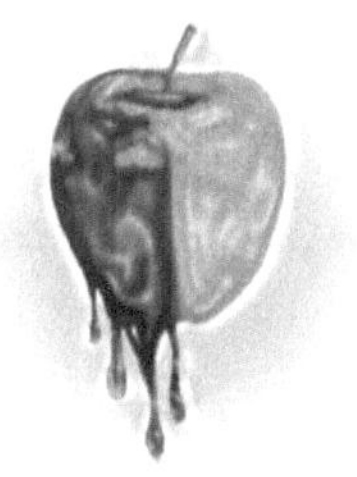

Chapter 31
A Prisoner

Shirayuki was not happy when I came to her chambers once the tower room was ready to be her new cage.

"What? Did someone tell the guards to not even speak to me?" she spat when I entered her room. "And what's with the locked door? Am I your prisoner now?"

Tears pricked my eyes.

"I do not wish for you to be a prisoner, Shirayuki, but you have to admit you're tying our hands here. Your brothers have to do what's best for everyone who lives in this house, not just you."

"What are you talking about?" This time her voice dripped with honey, but behind it I could still hear the venom ready to strike out.

"Come on Shirayuki, you're a smart girl, but even you know you wouldn't be able to hide your guilt forever, especially not from me or your brothers. I know you. And I know you killed those men." I crossed my arms across my chest, hoping she didn't see that they were trembling.

"Perhaps I should offer you the same fate," she spat in my face.

"I'm honestly a little surprised that you haven't yet. But the fact that my life is still intact tells me you're not in a hurry to do so. No, I think you want me to suffer first. Perhaps you were going to kill the whole town first and make me feel completely helpless to stop you, I don't know, but I am quite certain you don't intend to harm me... yet."

Shirayuki scoffed. "You know nothing."

"Really? I know that I will do everything in my power to make sure you don't hurt anyone else. And yes, that means making you a prisoner."

"You can certainly try." I hear a cracking noise and I'm left to wonder if that was her knuckles or some other joint that she might be stretching.

I tensed up, slipping a small vial out from the folds of my kimono and loosening the cork. I listen intensely for the sign of her attack. It's almost impossible. The only thing I hear is the pounding of the blood in my ears and the breath in my lungs. I tilt my head to the side, straining to hear anything- her breath, a footstep, anything.

Finally I hear it, a rustle of her clothes. I wait a full two seconds, and another, and then I feel the floorboards bend as she launches off them. I pop the cork all the way out and let it fall to the ground as I twist and throw the contents in the direction of her movements just moments before her body slams into me.

We crash to the ground and all of my breath escapes my lungs. I gasp for breath and end up inhaling the sleep power that is covering Shirayuki's face. I cough and push her off me.

"It's clear" I manage to call out before the drowsiness hits me and I collapse next to Shirayuki.

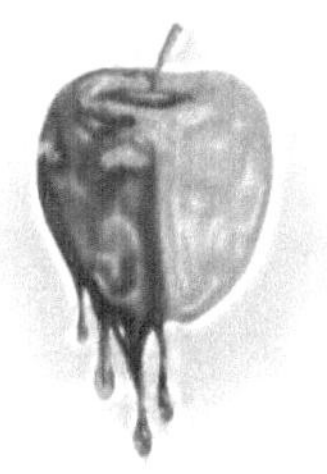

Chapter 32
Kagami's Return

I wake in my bed to a maid servant shuffling around my room. I know it's a maid servant because they tend to walk on the balls of their feet.

"Did they get Shirayuki moved to her new quarters?" I asked, and ended up coughing as my dry throat scratched at the words.

"Here." Kagekatsu was suddenly at my side, placing a glass in my hand.

He helped me sit up so I could drink and ease the ache in my throat.

"Thank you." I said handing him back the glass now drained of water. "Did Shirayuki make it to her new quarters?" I ask again.

"Yes, the captain wanted me to tell you that she made it to her new quarters and received her meal for the day, he also wanted you to know that everything went smoothly and she stayed asleep the whole time."

I nodded and fell back onto the bed. "Thank goodness."

"Sir Kagekatsu? Miss Yumi?" the maid servant Urakami spoke up.

"Hmm?" We responded in unison.

"Forgive me, this is none of my business but, Shirayuki, what is wrong with her?"

"I wish I knew," I said. "Unfortunately, I've never seen anything like it."

The maid is quiet before asking, "Is she contagious?"

"I don't think so. If she were, I think we would see more people exhibiting her symptoms."

"I should let you rest." Urakami says, "Do you need anything? Are you hungry?"

I open my mouth to speak but then I feel it, a warmth spread across my mind and a flicker of Kagami's tails in bursts of bright orange and red light sparks across my mind's eye.

"Um, no I'm good thank you, I think I'll just rest some more."

I listened as her footsteps retreated out the door.

"Perhaps I shall let you rest as well." Kagekatsu said once Urakami had left.

I gripped his hand before he could escape. "No stay. And close the door."

"Miss Yumi I —well, I don't think that— not that I don't-"

I interrupted his train of thought, my face burning, "Kagami is back, I just didn't want any staff walking by to overhear us. Or seeing Kagami speak freely with us for that matter."

"Oh right, of course." I let go of his hand to allow him to get up and heard the door slide closed.

"Kagami!?" I called.

"Yumi, you look terrible," she says as a warmth envelopes me. and I feel her body weight curl up onto my lap.

"It's good to see you too" I smile as her brilliant image shimmers to life in front of me before it disappears.

"I'm sorry I was gone so long. My sisters had never seen anything like what I described, and we decided to wait and watch to see if we could figure out anything more."

"And did you?" I ask.

"No. I'm sorry Yumi."

"Did you learn anything useful? Because I don't know what to do anymore."

"There are a few things we can try, purifying rituals and the like..." she ventured.

"But she isn't possessed. We would know if she was possessed." I protested.

"I mean it's worth a try, right?" Kagekatsu's voice was filled with desperation.

"You're right, I'll try after the funeral tomorrow."

I sat forward and hugged Kagami's warm form to me.

I'm sorry I was gone for so long. She whispered to just my mind.

It's okay, I think back to her, *I managed well enough.*

Sure, but it couldn't have been easy. I mean I left just one week after you found out Kenshin died. I feel like most mortals are still grieving, and you ended up having to deal with Shirayuki's whole mess.

Tears welled up in my eyes. A hard lump formed in my throat. It felt like years had passed since Kenshin's death. And yet we still hadn't given him a proper funeral; we were waiting for Shirayuki to be found, and then with her peculiar reappearance we wanted to wait to see if she would have the strength to come. Then guards started dropping and well, we were worried about assassins coming to the public viewing.

But now that we knew it was Shirayuki and she was better contained, it should be safe to do so. Kagekatsu and Kagetora didn't want to wait any longer to put their father to rest. I could hardly believe that it had only been two weeks since he died. It felt like an eternity had passed. So much had happened. So much loss, and it all started with him.

Have you spoken with Kagekatsu much since I left? Kagami asked.

No, I am afraid he will blame me for what's happened with his sister.

You know that's not true. If it was he wouldn't be here.

I know, I guess I'm afraid to tell him I don't know how to help her.

To be fair, no one does.

That doesn't really help me feel better.

Yeah but it might, one day.

I heaved a sigh and covered my face with my hands wiping my tears.

"I'm sorry Kagekatsu," I say.

"What for?"

"I'm supposed to be the resident expert on all things supernatural, but the forces Shirayuki was dealing with..." I trailed off.

"I'm sorry Yumi. I..." I felt the bedroll shift as he sat down next to me.

"What do you have to be sorry for?"

His calloused hand enveloped mine. "I didn't realize how much pressure you've been under. I know we are in uncharted territory. I know you are doing everything you can. I don't expect you to magically fix everything."

"Thanks Kagekatsu," I whispered, fresh tears rolling down my cheeks.

His free hand brushed my cheek, wiping a tear away. I leaned into his hand and closed my eyes, savoring this moment.

After a moment Kagekatsu cleared his throat. "I um, I should let you rest. I need to explain things to Kagetora about Shirayuki's new quarters." He let his hand drop from my cheek, leaving it cold. "He... isn't happy with me."

"Oh yes, of course I didn't mean to keep you from your family."

"Yumi," he squeezed my hand. "You are my family too." With that he walked out of my room. Stopping at the door he said, "Sweet dreams," and slid the door closed behind him.

I furrowed my brow, unsure of his meaning that I was family too. Wondering if I should take offense or not.

My feelings were a raging waterfall throughout our conversation, but at the end, I was plunged off the deep end, completely disoriented.

"Oh relax," Kagami yawned. "He's been in love with you since the moment he laid eyes on you. Now I'm going to bed, I'm tired."

I pushed her off my lap. "Not helping."

"What do you mean? I am very helpful!" Kagami protested.

"Whatever," I flopped onto the bed and buried my face into the covers.

Kagami curled up next to me. Her presence calmed my nerves more than her words did, and eventually I was able to drift back off to sleep.

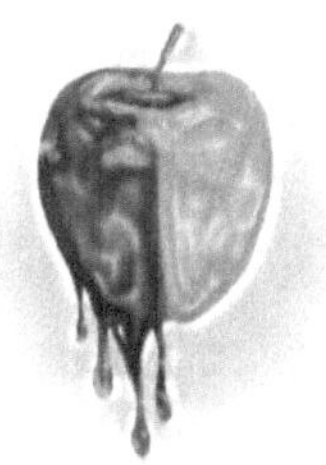

Chapter 33

An Itako Forever and Always

Shirayuki was in a sour mood the day of her adopted father's funeral.

Which was to be expected, but it was still heartbreaking. We couldn't very well let her attend. Kagekatsu agreed we didn't know enough about her condition. I didn't know if her appetite for blood was something she could control, or if she would go on a rampage throughout the mourning crowd, draining them one by one until we could contain her again. Regardless, we couldn't risk it. I tried to tell her this but she just screamed and began throwing furniture across her room, so I made a hasty exit and locked her door behind me. I could still hear her screams echoing through the halls of the castle as I returned to my room to prepare for the ceremony. Kagetora found me along the way

"Yumi, you really aren't going to let her come?"

"You saw what she did to the guards Kagetora, you know we can't let her near people. Not now."

He grunted, "She deserves to mourn our father."

"I agree. She does. But honestly I don't think that's Shirayuki anymore."

"How can you say that! Next you'll be calling for her head just like Kagekatsu!"

Tempers had run high among the two adopted brothers of Kenshin. They both were trying to succeed him. Though an all out war hadn't happened yet. I suspected it would arrive shortly after Kenshin was properly buried and put to rest. No doubt Shirayuki would be in on this as well, but we weren't letting her get the chance. No army of respectable samurai would follow a possessed leader. She would be on her own if she wanted to succeed Kenshin as daimyō.

"I am not even considering that. Not until I've tried everything in my power to get her back."

"Do you think that's possible?" He sounded so hopeful.

I bit my lip, "If it is, I haven't found a way yet.

But I won't stop trying."

"Thank you. And, I'm sorry for snapping at you. I suppose you're right about not being able to keep her restrained in a room full of people she could drain."

"I wish there was a way she could come. But that's not feasible right now. And we really shouldn't postpone this funeral any longer. We need to put his spirit to rest."

Kagetora didn't respond, but eventually his footsteps padded away along the wooden floors.

***

Dressed in my favorite kimono, I slung my black lacquered bamboo over my back and lifted my rosary of beads and bones over my head to rest around my neck. I took a deep breath.

Well look at you, I haven't seen you ready to face the spiritual realm in a long time. Kagami spoke in my mind, her presence pacing around me, taking in my look.

"It feels good to use them." I say referring to the bamboo and rosaries which have been a staple in my outfit ever since I became a full-fledged Itako. "I feel like myself again in a way."

I know you loved your life here with the Uesugi

family, and have let your Itako duties take second to being friends and keeping an eye on Shirayuki, but a part of you always was an Itako.

I take another shaky breath. "I know, it's time I get back to that part of myself, it might be the only way to save Shirayuki."

Kagami was silent. I knew she thought that Shirayuki was beyond saving. The purification rites I know hinge on connecting with the soul, which we can't find, which means there is nothing to purify. No possession seems to have taken place, we can't feel any presence in her. That's kind of the problem, so those solutions have been pointless to try. Aside from death, we are scrambling to find another solution.

A knock pulls me out of my thoughts and I turn towards the door. "Yes?" I called.

"It's time to go Miss Yumi. Are you ready?"

"Yes, let's go."

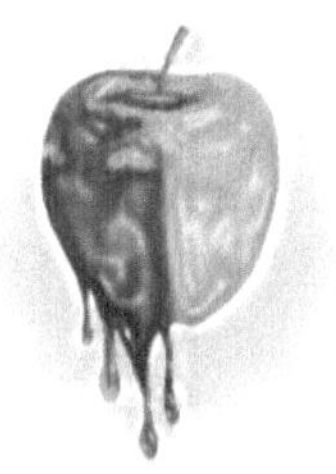

Chapter 34
The Funeral

I followed the sounds of the maid's footsteps as she led the way to Kenshin's resting place in the castle. When he first died, the staff and guards performed many of our traditions to keep his spirit safe until he was to be laid in his final resting place. These included his sons giving him his last taste of water, him being laid with his head north, and being brought his favorite meal twice a day.

Now it was time to transfer him to his final resting place. I knew that the priest performing the ceremony would be at the grave site now, purifying it in preparation for Kenshin's arrival.

We walked to the main courtyard and my ears were assaulted by the sounds of people bustling about. It was the people in the village, family, friends of Kenshin, his soldiers. They all milled about, waiting for the funeral to start.

Many came and offered condolences to the sons and asked how Shirayuki was doing. I couldn't keep anyone straight. I had too much on my mind. The room was loud and my head was spinning and all I could think about was Shirayuki's screams upstairs. I tried to follow the proceedings but Kagetora's words echoed in my mind as tears began to trace their way down my face. 'She deserves to attend our fathers funeral.'

A eulogy was given, prayers were said, rituals done to protect the spirit on its journey. Finally someone nudged me.

"What?" I asked, jumping in surprise.

"It's time to perform the kuchiyose ceremony." Kagekatsu, I think, is the one who spoke, his rough hands helping me up.

"Right," I let him pull me up and made my way to the front of the proceedings, blocking the coffin from the view of the grieving visitors.

Usually a body is laid to rest within six days from the time of death. But exceptions are made when necessary, like a child going missing and feral, for example.

I took a deep breath and faced the crowd.

Kagami leaned her side against my leg, letting me know she was there. Someone touched my arm and I reached out towards them as they placed two bowls in my hands. I knew these were filled with rice and salt. I set them down next to the coffin and dug my hands into the bowls grabbing fist-fulls of the contents and I began to chant. The words tumbled around in my head as I scattered the grains in my hands all about. At this point I was going through the motions of muscle memory, I probably looked to the audience like I was in a fever, but I was numb. I asked the gods to compel Kenshin to come to me, I asked the kami to protect those in attendance and all others to come witness. I sang songs to call Kenshin forward.

Soon enough I saw him. An ethereal blue shadowy spirit of Kenshin appeared before me. He looked young, like he had the day Kagami had showed me an image of him when we first met. His square jaw was clean-shaven and his long hair was tied in a loose ponytail, stray hairs fell framing his face. He wore his armor as if he were about to go to battle. It hugged his frame and he stood there for a second looking like he was about to command one of his generals to attack. But then he saw me. My breath hitched as a wave of guilt washed over me. I continued singing but in my head I had a private conversation with him first.

"Kenshin, I'm so sorry."

"You have nothing to apologize for. I should have warned you and given you more details about why I was so worried about Shirayuki."

"No! I'm sorry that I lost her hours after you were gone and now she is gone too. I-I don't know if I can help her.

Kenshin's eyes darkened, "Yes, I've seen what has become of her. I don't think anything can save her. She is too far gone."

"There must be something! I wish I knew more. I wish I knew what happened after Kagami lost trace of her soul."

"Shingen and I, we were watching her," Kenshin said carefully.

"Please you have to tell me, let me save your friend's daughter, your daughter."

Kenshin shook his head. "Dark magic. She was overtaken by some... thing... she summoned it up from the depths. A bird maybe, I couldn't tell, but it changed her. She transformed into that and her soul was gone. She fed on travelers and wild beasts until she decided to come home."

"But that doesn't make any sense. Why would she come back?"

I hadn't realized it, but at some point I had stopped singing, tears were beginning to roll down my cheeks. Kenshin's form flickered.

"Yumi we don't have time, you have to finish the ceremony."

I nodded and picked up the song again and his form resolidified in front of me.

"Thank you, Yumi. I know when the time comes you will be strong enough to do what needs to be done." He pressed his forehead to mine and then his spirit melded into me. The shock of cold overtook my body.

My song stopped. And Kenshin took hold of my vocal cords. He recounted his greatest battle with his rival Shingen and his favorite poem and the attending mourners asked him questions and he answered them. I listened as he used my body to set the minds of the mourners in attendance at ease and comforted them. Then I dismissed him. Warmth returned to my limbs as I sang more songs dismissing the spirits who had gathered and thanking the kami for protecting the mourners. I repeated the final song three times to finish the ceremony.

I stepped aside. My throat raw from all the singing and projecting my voice into the spiritual realm. Not to mention the lump that had formed along with my tears that I was failing to hold back. The room buzzed with murmured well wishes and tears as the guests came and said their final goodbyes to Kenshin. I stood behind Kenshin's two sons, out of the way, waiting for the proceedings to be over. Eventually, Kagetora and Kagekatsu placed Kenshin's sword on his chest and banners were put in place around his body to signal to his spirit that it was time to be moved.

The shuffle of feet and murmurs of those around me made it hard to distinguish which footfalls were the guards who carried Kenshin out of the room. Next I was to perform the purification ceremony hakkyu-go batsujonogi[24] on the home, but I wanted nothing more than to follow Kenshin to his final resting place. To stay beside Kagekatsu and support him, but he was going on ahead of me. I was about to begin the purification ritual when I was stopped cold by a blood curdling scream.

---

[24] **Hakkyu-go Batsujonogi** /ha-**kyu** go **ba**-su-joh-noh-gee / the act of purifying the home after the body is removed from where the funeral took place.

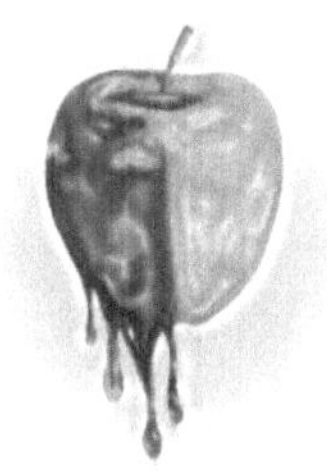

Chapter 35
Secrets Unveiled

The mourners began frantically running to the exit and pushed past me as I stood in the middle of the room trying to grasp at the fractured conversations I heard from the people pushing and shoving past me. Dizzy and disoriented from the panicked crowd I gripped my head and tried to focus on their words, not the incoherent screaming and the slamming of their feet on the pavement.

"Did you see her?"

"Was that blood?"

"What is happening?"

"She just threw them across the room like it was nothing"

"Blood everywhere, I couldn't tell who was hurting who."

"Do you think she's gone mad?"

"She wasn't here earlier."

"I heard they locked her in a tower."

I gritted my teeth and turned against the crowd which was thinning now as most of the people had moved away from Shirayuki.

"Shirayuki?" I called aloud but mentally I called my kitsune. *Kagami, tell me what's happening.*

Stupid people trampled me, stepped on my beautiful tail, when this is over I'll show them who-

Kagami, I cut her grumbling off. *I think I'm going to need your help here.*

"Yumi, Yumi, Yumi." Shirayuki's voice crooned.

The crowd had either all left or was silently watching because by the time Shirayuki had finished speaking my name the room was deathly silent.

I heard the loud thud of a body being dropped to the ground.

I count four dead. She attacked quickly, snapping their necks or knocking them out so she would have time to drain them completely later before too many people ran out of reach. Someone tried to stop her, a guard, but she slit his throat with his own blade. She is about ten paces away now, standing in the entrance to the hallway that leads to the kitchen.

Four dead. I wondered who they were, if I knew them, but I knew Kagami wouldn't tell me until after this was over, she would want me to stay focused. I moved to take a step toward her but a hand on my arm stopped me.

"Aw, and my dear brothers have come to play as well."

"Shirayuki, why have you done this?" The voice came from my right and slightly behind. It was Kagetora.

"I asked nicely if I could come," Shirayuki sang in a soft singsong voice.

"And we told you since you couldn't control your appetite you were to stay in your room." I said.

"Aw, but you brought such a wonderful feast. I simply couldn't resist." I heard her step forward lightly on the wooden floor. And two swords, one on either side of me, were immediately drawn by her brothers.

"Go back to your room, you're not welcome

here," Kagekatsu said in his most commanding voice.

"You care to fight me brothers? I hope you brought your army. Because I'm stronger than you can possibly imagine."

"Do you happen to have any more of that sleeping powder on your person?" Kagetora asked me under his breath.

"Oh, you're no fun," Shirayuki pouted before I could respond. "Trying to sedate me, a coward's route. You know Kenshin taught us the only way to win a war was through battle, not underhanded tricks." The boys shifted uncomfortably next to me.

They knew all too well what their father had thought of underhanded tricks. He once helped Shingen out, sending the Kai province supplies when Nobunaga had cut off trade routes. Even though it would have benefited Kenshin to let his rival suffer and weaken, he helped instead, saying that if he was going to beat his opponents it would be on the battlefield, not with dirty tricks. He was a man of honor and integrity.

"I can hear you plotting through the walls," she sang and let out a cackle. "I know what you wish to do to me and I know who is still loyal even if they refuse to let me go free."

My hands trembled. Could she really know? Could she know that Kagekatsu was beginning to agree with Koga who thought it best to kill her but that Kagetora and I held him back?

Fresh tears poured down my face, "Please Shirayuki, please. Just go back upstairs. I don't want to lose any more friends trying to get you back upstairs."

"I AM NOT YOUR PRISONER "

"No," Kagekatsu said. "But you're not my sister either. You've always had ruthless battle strategies, but this? This useless killing, and for what? You've become a monster Shirayuki."

"You're pathetic," I heard her spit.

"I don't want to believe you're past saving Shirayuki, I don't. But even Kenshin believes you're too far gone." I said, choking on my words, not wanting to admit the truth. My throat aches as a lump forms at its base. "I'm sorry that I don't know how to stop this, but you're giving us no choice. It's us or you. And if we let you live you'll soon drink your way through Echigo."

"I thought you would never abandon me Yumi," Shirayuki sneered.

My heart felt like it was being ripped in two. "Please, just go to your room. Maybe, maybe I can still find a way to reverse this."

"Reverse?" She laughed. "Why would I want to reverse this?" A crash sounded across the room. I flinched wondering what she made crumble with a single blow. "I am the strongest being in all of Nihon! I don't need you or your pity of what I've become. And I won't need anyone ever again. Well, except maybe their blood I suppose," she trailed off.

She is wondering if she could reach a bystander cowering in the corner to feed off them. She still isn't satisfied from her meal earlier. Kagami whispered.

"Don't even think about it." I said, stepping forward.

In an instant she was on me. Her body pressed against mine in an embrace.

"Yumi!" Kagekatsu shouted. But he couldn't strike her or he'd hit me. I should have told him to. It would've been worth it if she had died right then.

Kagami growled.

"You have a good supply of blood," Shirayuki whispered in my ear. "It's pumping very fast through your veins, almost like it's reaching out for me to take." She whimpered as she placed her lips to my neck.

I shuddered at her touch.

After a moment she pulled back, her teeth never making contact with my skin.

"Of course I'd never drink your blood. It's tainted. Too much magic. Too many dead spirits." I felt her hair brush across the side of my face as she vigorously shook her head. "No, too gross to even consider. Not that it doesn't smell delightful," she moaned and brushed her lips against my skin as she spoke. "I sometimes wonder if your witchcraft might make you taste even sweeter, but I've decided it would be better to have you and my brothers survive this whole ordeal. I can destroy everything you love and make you feel completely powerless to stop it."

She pushed me away from her and I stumbled back. Kagekatsu caught me and steadied me in his free arm.

"Now, are we going to fight? Are you just going to stand there with your swords drawn like idiots? I will warn you though, if you bleed, I might not be able to control myself despite what I said about wanting you to live to see everything crumble around you."

When I say now, grab the brothers and pull them away. And usher any bystanders outside the compound while you are at it. Kagami tells me im my mind.

Okay.

A hoard of footsteps poured into the room from every hallway that led out of the room. It sounded like an entire army had come to our aid. I stayed put, trusting Kagami's timing.

"Aw I'm flattered! You think you need an army to stop me? I'll dispose of them quickly."

Kagekatsu growled in frustration, his sword clicked as he adjusted his grip.

Okay now!

As she spoke the room erupted in chaos, I turned and grabbed the brothers' arms and ushered them out of the room.

They protested and fought against my grip until I hissed "It's an illusion."

"What?" Kagetora said, for a moment I had forgotten that he didn't know about Kagami.

"Just come on!" Kagekatsu said, ushering him onward and shouting at bystanders to get out of the building.

We urged them to go home or to the grave site if they still wanted to and stood with our army outside the castle listening to the sounds of battle.

"What army is in there if we are all out here?" Kagetora asked.

"Shh. Not here, I'll explain later when less people are about."

Kagekatsu put his arm around me and held me.

"You guys are keeping secrets from me," Kagetora said, disappointment clearly evident in his voice.

"I know you've always been close to Shirayuki," I said carefully, "I, didn't want you to tell her certain things."

Kagetora scoffed.

The smell of smoke drifted up to my nose.

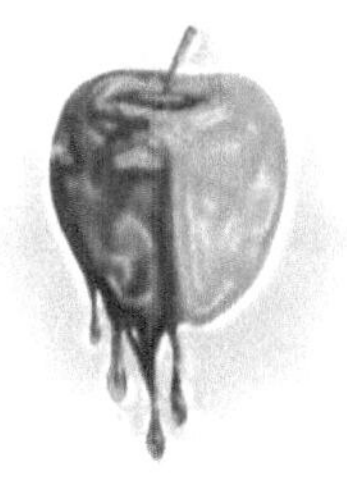

Chapter 36
Tokiwa

"Is the castle on fire?" I asked frantically.

"No, at least not that I can tell. It might not have spread to the outside yet," Kagekatsu said.

Come now Yumi, you know I have more self-control than that. Kagami chided in my mind from inside the pagoda.

I took a deep breath and tried to relax.

Show me, I told her.

Seriously? You hate it when I project images into your mind.

Yeah well I'm going crazy not knowing what is happening.

Alright, you asked for it.

Kagami projected a bird's eye view of the scene happening inside the pagoda. The imaginary army was gone and a few plumes of smoke rose from pieces of furniture that were now charred. Kagami glowed, her reddish orange coat gleaming with power, her seven tails swishing as she rubbed them together and they lit on fire. The fire was blinding and Shirayuki hissed as she shrank away from the light, shielding her eyes. Kagami stalked towards her and she stumbled into the hallway.

"Kagami!" Shirayuki gasped, "I thought we were friends. Can't we just talk?" She was dressed for training in a flowery kimono with long drooping sleeves and black hakama[25] pants. Her sword was not at her waist so I assumed it was still hanging on the training center's wall. She didn't retrieve it before attacking.

"No." Kagami growled. "You don't touch Yumi and think you'll get away with it."

"Yumi, Yumi, Yumi," she whined, "It's always Yumi, Yumi's magic is good, but when I try, I get put in isolation!"

Kagami's fire burned brighter in response. And Shirayuki hissed again. That's when I noticed her

---

[25] **Hakama** /ha-**kah**-mah/ - loose trousers with many pleats in the front, worn over the kimono. Frequently worn by samurai.

teeth. She had two long fangs on her upper and lower teeth that looked like they belonged on a canine.

Kagami had her stumbling up the winding stairs that would lead up to the top floor where her tower room was.

"Come on," Shirayuki complained. "I get it, you're powerful, but seriously you are wasting your time bonding with that Itako. Imagine the mischief we could make just you and me."

"That Itako is my friend. I would never betray her, even for a bit of mischief."

"Oh it'd be more than a bit," Shirayuki was still steadily walking backwards up the stairs, her hand out as if trying to tame a wild animal.

"Okay, let me rephrase, no amount of mischief."

Shirayuki stumbled as they emerged on another floor before they continued their assent up. I could hear Shirayuki's thoughts as she scrambled for an escape plan.

Soon though they emerged on the top floor of the pagoda. Shirayuki's door was shattered and the guards who had been on duty during the funeral were slumped on the ground, their skin as pale as

Shirayuki's. I noticed a bite mark on one of their necks.

I faintly heard someone calling my name but I ignored them.

Kagami backed Shirayuki into the room and onto her bedroll in the corner.

"How will you keep me here Kagami? The door is gone. And I doubt you can stand guard here forever. Yumi will get lonely."

Kagami's only response was a throaty growl and her fire burning hotter.

Shirayuki shrank back shielding her black soulless eyes.

Then in a flash of white light a second kitsune stood beside Kagami. Her fur was pure white with red markings on her face, ears, paws and tails, all nine of them. Shriayuki's eyes widened and then she froze. Kagami relaxed and let her fire die. Shirayuki stayed frozen.

The white kitsune sat, her tails swirling around her majestically.

"You have about two hours. " she said lazily, "that's how long I'll tolerate being helpful," she began licking her front paws and the vision dissolved from my mind. I quickly turned to

Kagekatsu, tugging on his kimono

"We need to hurry and fortify her room. We only have two hours."

"What? Yumi, what are you talking about?" he asked.

"She broke her doors, we need wood and nails and anything sturdy to keep her locked away. Enough to cover all the windows and her doorway. Quickly!"

Kagekatsu hurried off shouting instructions to a few guards.

Kagetora remained still.

"Why is everyone frozen but us and a few guards?" Kagetora asked eventually.

"Kagami called in a favor," I said grimly.

"Kagami? Your pet?"

"She's more than a pet. Now come on, we only have two hours, we need to hurry."

I took off towards the pagoda and hurried to the stairs. I could hear Kagetora close behind me. When we reached the top floor Kagetora gasped.

"Nakamikado, Honjou!" He pushed past me to his fallen comrades.

"Yeah, Shirayuki must have killed them when she broke down the door."

"They didn't even get a chance to draw their blades," he said.

I paused, I hadn't noticed that their blades were still sheathed when I was watching Kagami shepherd Shirayuki into the room. I stepped carefully around the bodies and the wreckage from memory of what I saw when I was watching Kagami, and entered Shriayuki's new room.

"Well, well, well, if it isn't the precious human girl that Kagami is so fond of," a malevolent voice spoke from the center of the room.

Kagami circled my legs in a tight formation, letting her tails fan out and curl around me. I leaned down and placed a hand on her neck, stroking her gently.

After a moment, Kagami spoke.

"Yumi, meet my sister, Tokiwa," she said begrudgingly.

I heard multiple gasps and I assumed that Kagekatsu, along with the few men that hadn't been frozen in time, had arrived with the supplies necessary for securing her.

"I like your friends Yumi," Tokiwa said softly.

"They know how to show respect to a powerful deity."

"You're no deity" Kagami grumbled.

I turned slightly to the men behind me. "Enough of that," I said, "hurry, we don't have much time."

The room filled with the noise of hammers on nails as the men began boarding up the windows. When they had finished with that, we all left the room so they could close up the doorway. I stood at the end of the hallway out of the way, with the two kitsune.

"You know this counts as your one favor," Tokiwa said.

"I know," Kagami grumbled.

"I was surprised to hear your plea for help so soon, and it wasn't even to kill the wretched girl. You still could you know."

"We won't kill her unless it's our only option," I said firmly.

Kagami sighed deeply and laid her head on one of my feet.

Her sister laughed, "I think it already is, but whatever, you can have it your way. I did my part.

Don't come crying to me when more people start dying and you wish you would have killed her off now. You're on your own."

"I know," I said.

"I wish I could convince you to let me stay just for a while. Those men look delicious." Tokiwa whispered loudly.

"Don't even think about it," I said, gripping my rosary.

"Honestly Kagami, I don't know how you can stand it being so close to so many strapping young men and not try to seduce them." Tokiwa moaned.

"Maybe I'm more mature than you are," Kagami said quietly.

"What was that?"

"Nothing."

She sighed. "You sure I can't convince you to let me possess you Yumi? I could have Kagekatsu in your bed in no time.

Heat flooded to my cheeks. The bones on my rosary threatened to cut me as my grip on them tightened.

"Don't even think about it. You will leave here and not bother any of these men when your task is done.

"Aww, you're no fun," she sighed again, "But I suppose I'll do as you ask. I don't really want to get on an Itako's bad side. Not that you could actually harm me, but you could be incredibly annoying for a few years before you died off. And it's not worth it right now.

Kagekatsu's voice called out as he walked towards me, "Yumi, they will be done in just a few more minutes." He rested his hand on my shoulder and I flinched at the contact.

"Are you okay?" he asked.

"Yes!" I moved my arm and his hand fell to his side. I rubbed my head trying to get Tokiwa's words out of it.

"It's good you're almost done, Kagekatsu," Tokiwa mused. "Your two hours will be up soon."

"I was wondering about that, why only two hours?" he asked.

"Cuz I felt like it," she said simply.

Kagekatsu didn't have a response to that.

The rest of the men made their way over to us as the last of the pounding of the hammers and nails faded away. I heard the rustle of their hakama as they knelt in reverence in the presence of the two kitsune who sat beside me.

Tokiwa simply said, "You're two hours will be up in ten minutes."

Then in a blindly white flash she disappeared. I blinked against the brightness until my eyesight returned to its normal dark and fuzzy state.

"We should get back downstairs and escort anyone else to the grave site," I said. "I'll perform the purification ritual before I head there myself."

I straightened the strap of my bamboo on my shoulder and turned to head downstairs.

Murmurs followed me as the men marveled about what had just happened. I heard some of them say Kagami's name and I felt her pride bubble up inside me.

You did good, I told her.

Thanks, I'm lucky she doesn't like light, or else my fire wouldn't have done much.

So, your sister... I ventured.

Ugh I wish I didn't need to call her, but my strength is in fire, not time. I wouldn't have been able to buy you two full hours. It would have been an hour at most. And I doubt I could have done that long.

You made the right call. I told her

Thanks, I just hope that holds her. We can't have her running loose in the city.

No, that would be very bad, I agreed.

I bit my lip as I thought again of what I could possibly do to change her back. Nothing came to mind.

I reached the main hall where the funeral was held and started the purification ritual. When I was done Kagami brushed against my side and I leaned down to pet her.

"I can escort you to the grave site," Kagekatsu said from the corner of the room.

"Oh, I thought you would have gone ahead," I frowned.

"That's okay. I kind of wanted to be here when our ten minutes were up."

"How much time do we have now?" I asked.

"Everything should unfreeze any second now."

There was a beat of silence before it was broken by a scream.

I flinched.

I heard Kagekatsu prepare to draw his sword.

A faint pounding sounded on the door we boarded up, but it soon stopped as another wordless scream ripped through the air. Then all was quiet.

"I think she is done for now," Kagekatsu said after a bit. "She will want to formulate a new strategy before she tries to break out again."

I nodded and turned to walk toward the outside. After a moment Kagekatsu grabbed my hand and looped it in his arm so he could guide me to the gravesite.

The rest of the funeral went smoothly and Kenshin was able to be placed in his final resting place, though the crowd was filled with whispers and rumors of what had happened back at the house. Most of them ran home before they saw too much, but some had stayed huddled in a corner and watched. The reports of what happened varied wildly, forming a confusing picture of today's events.

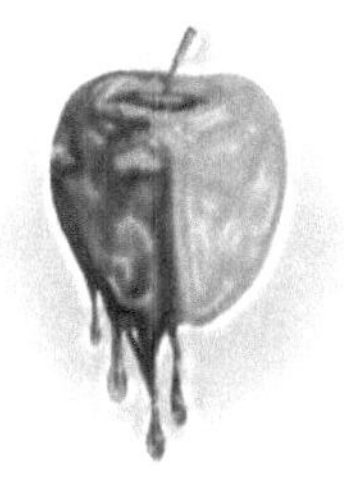

Chapter 37
Unkillable

A few weeks went by and Shirayuki was quiet; however, the house was anything but. Once their father was laid to rest, Kagekatsu and Kagetora spend most of their time fighting, trying to prove who is the strongest and most eligible to replace Kenshin as Daimyō.

They were evenly matched for the most part, and the rest of the army was hesitant to take sides. But eventually in one of their sparring matches, Kagekatsu bested Kagetora, and the fight ended with Kagetora committing seppuku[26] once he realized his defeat.

The mourning period for Kagetora was short. Too much time was wasted on family affairs as it

---

[26] **Seppuku** /seh-**puu**-kuu/ the honorable method of taking one's own life practiced by samurai in feudal Japan.

was. Nobunaga's armies were closing in, claiming territories on our borders in our distraction. But I knew Kagetora's death broke something in Kagekatsu. While in the recent past they had grown apart; differing opinions on the war effort and how to deal with Shirayuki, even before Kenshin's death meant they argued regularly. But Kagekatsu often would tell me stories of them training together and getting into mischief when they were younger.

With Kagetora's death, especially so soon after Kenshin's, and Shirayuki's... new addiction to blood, I didn't know how much more tragedy he could take. He acted the part of daimyō; he was strong for the men he led, a grounding point in the confusion and grief that overtook them as these events ceaselessly pounding their morale into the dirt.

But when no one was around, Kagekatsu would often heave a heavy sigh, and his strong arm around me would droop, his stature losing all sense of posture. And he would weep into my shoulder as I held him up. Being his rock when he didn't have to be everyone else's.

***

It wasn't until the day after Kagetora's funeral that we realized that Shirayuki had escaped.

Three guards were found dead in the gardens, drained of their blood. Her sword from the training room was missing, along with her tessen, and another guard was found dead not too far from there. Her door was the same, still boarded up. The men had to pry off the boards to search her room. We hadn't gone in there since boarding it up. Not even to bring her food. I didn't think she needed it anyways. Her new diet consisted purely of blood.

Her window had the boards pried off. Kagekatsu guessed she broke out then slipped into another window, grabbed her sword, and left out through the kitchen's backdoor that led to the garden.

As he told me what they found, I sank to my knees.

"You were right," tears poured freely down my cheeks. "We should have killed her when we had the chance."

Soon after that, Kagekatsu left to find his sister.

***

Kagekatsu had been gone for a little more than two weeks. I sent Kagami with him to make sure he would come back alive. He went to find Shirayuki and kill her. I spent my days pacing in my room. I hardly ate, I was so sick with worry. Many reports came in from the guards telling of missing people who had gone into the woods and never returned. Some were found not far from the path through the mountains completely drained of their blood, others were never to be seen again. I was terrified of one of them coming back saying that Kagekatsu was among them.

The guilt of all those people dying because I didn't let them kill her when we had a chance, it was almost too much to bear. It ate away at my stomach, churning its contents, making me nauseous. No matter how much I tell myself of my reasons or my good intentions, it doesn't change the fact that Shirayuki wasn't me. She chose this path and was past the point of no return. She needed to be stopped by any means necessary.

***

Finally, as I paced my room late one night too worried to sleep, I felt a warmth rush through my limbs and a familiar voice rush to my mind.

We're back.

I flew out my bedroom door faster than I'd ever done before and raced down the halls till I burst out into the courtyard.

"Yumi!" Kagekatsu seemed surprised to see me.

I ran towards him barreling into his arms. He smelled richly of blood.

"I'm so sorry," he whispered into my hair as he held me. "I- I failed."

My heart felt like it stopped in my chest. I stiffened in his arms, fear rooting me to the place where I stood. I realized at that moment that we made yet another terrible mistake.

She wasn't human anymore. I mean, she drank blood for goodness sakes. Kagami didn't even think she had a heart beat. How do you kill something that's —for all intents and purposes— is dead already?

"Tell me what happened."

Kagekatsu began recounting his journey. I could tell he was exhausted; he probably wanted nothing more than to rest in his own bed after sleeping in the woods for weeks. But still he stayed and told me everything he could about Shirayuki.

"She is incredibly fast. You could see her in the distance and within seconds she could be right in front of you. This made it impossible to duel her. Her swordplay and techniques have become unrivaled with her new speed. And if I did manage to counter her blade, she hardly noticed. She seems to have the strength of 100 men. She could have overpowered me in seconds but she just laughed, saying I was nothing and that she wanted me to stay alive to watch everything Kenshin had worked for crumble to pieces."

I nodded, "she said the same to me."

"I did manage to sneak up on her while she was sleeping one day. I struck fast and aimed to cut out her heart. But, it's like she hardly even felt it. Her eyes opened and the black void stared up at me in horror for just a moment before she pulled my blade out. I watched as her skin knit itself back together. She threw the Katana away from her and hissed at me, saying 'now you know that I'm unkillable' and then just sat there laughing. That's when I made my way back home."

I was trembling by the time he finished.

"You should go and rest. We can figure out what to do in the morning," I finally said.

"Okay," he slumped against me as exhaustion hit him a little harder.

I let him lean on me as I walked him to his chambers. I had just eased him onto his bedroll and was about to leave when he caught my hand.

"It's not your fault Yumi."

I turned my head away from him letting my

loose hair fall in front of my face.

With his other hand he pulled aside my curtain of hair. "Listen to me," he murmured, sleep attempting to win over his consciousness, "nobody could have stopped this. But we will figure it out. Together. Me and you."

I bit my lip, unsure of what to say. But it didn't matter anyways because his breathing deepened and his hand fell from my face with a heavy thud. I pulled my hand from his grasp and snuck out of the room, quietly sliding the door shut before collapsing in my own bedroll down the hall, Kagami's comforting form curled up beside me.

Chapter 38
Plotting

The next morning, I woke to a soft knock at my door. I rubbed the sleep from my eyes and squinted against the light streaming in through my window. Kagami was no longer curled up beside me.

"Come in," I called.

"Good morning Yumi," Kagekatsu said as he stepped inside my room, sliding the door shut behind him. His bare feet padded across the floor and he sat down beside me on the bedroll. He smelled of soap, so I knew he must have bathed the blood off this morning before coming to my door.

I was silent for a long time before I finally spoke.

"More than ten people dead at the hand of a thirteen year old girl who just wanted a meal." I sighed and laid back on my bed in defeat.

"How can we kill her?" Kagekatsu asked.

"I don't know if there is a way to kill her, but I'll look into it."

"I can have some men go out looking for answers as well.

"No. Our borders are already weakened. Nobunaga has already taken almost every other province in our distraction. We can't let him get any stronger. You should focus on the war. I'll deal with Shirayuki."

Kagekatsu hesitated, "Are you sure?"

"Yes. She's a demon, I'm an Itako. It's my job to rid the world of her. I'll figure it out."

"Still, I don't like the idea of you going after her alone. "

"I won't be, I'll have Kagami," I smiled up at him.

"Where is Kagami?"

I sighed, "I don't know, hopefully not getting into mischief."

Kagami, I called to her.

Immediately I felt her warm presence fill me up

inside. Her head rested on my lap and I patted her head.

Kagekatsu gasped at her sudden appearance out of thin air.

"Where have you been?" I asked.

"I was just looking around for some information in Shirayuki's old room. I was wondering if those books of dark magic told of a way to reverse or kill what she had become."

"Any luck?" Kagekatsu asked hopefully.

"No, it was spectacularly unhelpful. Though I do have an idea."

I sat up straighter. "What?"

"Well, when I was cornering her in the pagoda, she didn't like fire, that's the only time I saw fear in her eyes. Also when we were hunting her, she seemed to only rest during the day, and she would always find a shaded place to wait out the day."

"You think she doesn't like the light?" I asked.

"I'm wondering if we could burn her." Kagami confirmed. "I didn't mention it with Kagekatsu because I was worried I would start a forest fire, but, if we waited for her to settle somewhere, we could corner her and burn her. "

"Hmmm," Kagekatsu said thoughtfully, "that might work. It's worth a shot. "

"So, now we just wait for her to stop running and ambush her?" I asked.

"Yes, if we could sneak up on her and restrain her before we set her on fire, then we wouldn't have to worry about it spreading as much as it would in an all out fight."

I nodded. "Yes. This is good, we could do this."

"I suppose that's settled then," Kagekatsu said. "When do we head out? "

I frowned, "I think you should stay here to defend Echigo. We don't know when we will leave, or when Nobunaga will strike."

"I just don't like the thought of you going off to kill my unkillable sister alone."

"Kagami will make sure I return safely. If I've had to sit and worry about you going off to battle for the last few years and who knows how many more to come, you can do the same for me," I said.

"Okay, but promise you won't leave just yet. I want to spend some time with you before..." he trailed off but I knew what he meant. We were both going off to war soon.

I nodded and rested my head on his shoulder, "Sure, Kagami needs to figure out where Shirayuki is going to settle and what she is planning, anyways."

"Why do I have to do all the dirty work?" Kagami asked.

"Cuz you can spot her easily when you slip into the spirit realm," I pointed out.

"Still, you could at least have asked."

I rolled my eyes, "Kagami, could you spy on Shirayuki and keep tabs on her and help us defeat her when the opportunity arises?" I asked.

"Why of course, anything for you Yumi, you know you don't need to ask."

Kagekatsu laughed as I groaned at Kagami for being so insufferable.

When his laughter subsided and we fell into a long silence he cleared his throat, shifting uncomfortably.

"So, I've been meaning to talk to you, and I suppose now is as good of a time as any."

I shifted on my bedroll giving him my full attention.

Kagami climbed into my lap and curled into a

ball, whispering. *This is going to be good.*

I ignored her.

"I know you only came here by the request of Kenshin to befriend and help Shirayuki not give in to her more... uh... bloodthirsty tendencies."

"A feat I seem to have been failing at, yes I'm aware." I groaned, not liking the serious tone in his voice. He was going to send me away for failing, for losing his sister to the darkness, especially now that Kagetora is dead, he will be blaming me for not saving the only family he has left.

"And I know that you left your family behind to come here, your village, your friends... but I-"

"I know I've overstayed my welcome." I cut him off, "I just had hoped I could stay and see this whole issue with Shirayuki resolved."

"I... no. That is not what I was saying at all. Hold on let me start over, and get to the end too perhaps, I-" he took a deep breath before continuing. "I know you only came by request of Kenshin, and with him being gone and the end of his request in sight you might feel as though you no longer have a place here, and perhaps wish to finally return home.

"But, over the time you have stayed here, you

have become a part of our family. More so than I wanted to admit and I had hoped to ask, that once you feel your duty with Shirayuki is finished, if you would consider staying here a while longer." He paused and I could hear his hands rub the fabric of his hakama. "With me."

"Oh." Relief washed over me. Just last night in his sleepless delirium he had said we would figure this out together, then at the thought of him wishing for me to leave I panicked putting the words in his mouth so I wouldn't have to hear him say them. But he didn't want that, and my heart warmed at the thought. "Of course I can stay, if you think that my services will still be needed here. I'll gladly extend my stay."

Oh, you have got to be kidding me. I again ignored Kagami.

Kagekatsu however took a while to respond. His breath catching a few times as if he were about to speak and thinking better of it. I furrowed my brow, worried I might have said something wrong.

Finally, he said, "right, well. I better go."

"Okay," I said as he stood and walked to my door.

His footsteps paused at the door, he didn't slide it open though.

"Actually, no." Kagekatsu turned and walked back towards me, his form towering over me blocking out the light from the window. "I don't want Yumi the Itako to stay for the castle or the town's benefit. I want you. To stay I mean, I want you to stay but only if you wish, and I want you to stay for me."

I felt my eyes go wide and my mouth drop.

I told you so, Kagami taunted.

"I- I- uh" I blinked and shook my head hoping the act would bring me back to reality. "I would like that." I finally said. "To stay for you. I mean."

Kagekatsu's towering shadow sank to the ground in front of me.

"You know, I think Kagami is rubbing off on you a little too much. That wasn't fair." Relief was evident in his voice.

"Oh no, she was being serious," Kagami put in. "I kept trying to tell her, but she stayed stubbornly oblivious to your advances. I honestly am sorry for you."

Kagekatsu gave a hesitant laugh, "Well that makes me feel a little better." Then he reached out and grabbed my hand, lifting it to his lips. His hot breath brushed my knuckles as he spoke so softly I could barely hear him, "Please know this Yumi. Everything I want in this world is all encompassed in you." His lips brushed my knuckles as he punctuated this with a kiss before slowly placing my hand back onto Kagami's fur and walking away. Only pausing before sliding my door shut to say, "I'll see you at breakfast then?"

All I could manage to do in that moment was nod and breathe a single word, "Yes."

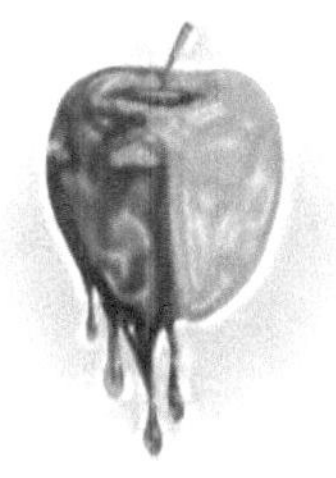

Chapter 39
An Imaginary Note

Shirayuki was living in the mountains with seven young miners. She told them a half truth about running away from her family who was trying to lock her up and when she escaped they sent someone after her to take her heart back to her cruel sister.

She had tattered her clothes and rubbed dirt and animal blood all over her. Of course any one would help a scared little girl covered in blood with a story like that. She settled into their cottage and cleaned up after them as repayment for their kindness, and at night she would sneak out and find some fresh blood to fill her belly.

The rumor of a monster in the mountains who preys on travelers grew. At first we thought it was only for those who traveled near our town, but soon anyone who traveled over the western mountains were warned of a beast who would devour anyone who strayed too far from their campfire at night. Many people went missing, later found dead. Meanwhile, I spent most waking hours trying to come up with a plan so we could hide from her while traveling and how to best corner her when we found her. Kagekatsu helped a little, and I helped him with plans for defending Echigo providence as best I could. Both of us keep our minds busy with the problems at hand instead of dwelling on all we had lost.

Soon enough, we both knew we had to go separate ways. He would soon leave to reinforce our troops. And it was time I found Shirayuki before the winter months hit. She had settled in quite nicely in her mountain home with those miners, but I had a feeling she wouldn't stay put forever. Kagami and I needed to make our move before she moved on.

We decided that Kagami would disguise me with an illusion of invisibility at night, and when we arrived at the cottage, I would appear as a frail old woman. I packed my bag with supplies I might need for the journey. I also brought a new kimono for Shirayuki, as a guise to let me get close as I offered it to her. From what Kagami had shown me, her own kimono was now tattered from her nightly hunts through the forest.

Kagami? I called.

I'm here, she said, brushing her back along my leg.

Are you ready to go?

Yes, but don't you think you should say goodbye to Kagekatsu?

I took a deep breath. *If I say goodbye then I might never leave.*

I slung my bag across my back along with my lacquered bamboo that held my Itako papers. I made my way through the pagoda as quietly as I could, and when I emerged I asked. *Show me Shirayuki.* My mind flooded with an image of Shirayuki, fair and beautiful as ever in her torn and patched kimono. She was walking back to the cottage, humming as she weaved her way through the wash that was on the line to dry. She looked peaceful and happy. When she approached the house, she glanced over and checked her appearance in the window's reflection. She bared her teeth, and her fangs came into full view. They were stained with blood. She walked over to the well and rinsed her mouth till her teeth were pure white again.

The image faded.

How do I get there? I asked.

Head left out of town. Kagami sighed, *You know, if you go missing, he might send people looking for you.*

I paused. *Could you leave him a note?*

An imaginary one, sure.

Just as long as it's there long enough for him to read it, I tell her before I continue walking through the empty streets of the town. Light is just barely beginning to brighten the sky along my back. The air is still wet with morning dew, and I don't pass anyone as I walk . Once I reach the town's edge I hesitate, waiting for Kagami to let me know where to go next.

"About thirteen paces to your right there is a path heading away from town." She speaks aloud. So there really must be nobody around.

I follow her instructions. I don't generally hike through the woods, there are many obstacles for me to traverse with little way for me to know when to step over or around them. Once I have tripped and stumbled on the roots about five times and get whacked in the face about another six times, Kagami asks if I'm ready to head back home.

"No," I shouted out loud. "I'm not going

home. I can do this. I just need something to hang on to like a walking stick. Do you see something that could work?"

I heard her audible sigh in my mind before responding. "Yeah go back three paces and then left four, there is a big stick, but you're going to have trouble getting to it."

Grumbling about how it would be so much easier if she would just hand it to me, I turned and headed backwards three paces and turn towards the stick. I know this will be veering off the path, which I was having a hard enough time navigating, but I take a deep breath and step carefully forward. Once I've found a good spot for my foot between the bushes and underbrush I reach out for a tree or branch and am able to find one after a moment. I grasp the tree and use it to steady myself as I bring my other foot to join the first. Just three more paces to go.

Once I finally get over to where the stick is supposed to be I begin to grope around until I find a branch laying on the ground.

"Is this what you meant?" I ask.

"Yes."

"I suppose it will have to do," I mumble to myself.

I sat down and began stripping all of the extra branches off of it so I can use it how I intend to. Once I'm satisfied, I stick it in the ground and use it to help me back up. Then carefully make my way back to the path. With my stick leading the way, warning me if there is a root or if the path turns, I fall much less often.

I walk until I feel like I can't walk any more. Then I rest and eat some food before continuing on. And when I get to the point that my legs feel like jelly, I take out the bedroll and sleep. When I wake up, Kagami has me continue on the trail to the west mountains. I spend the entire day walking. I get better with using the stick as a guide to feel for obstacles in my way. Though, occasionally it will get caught on a root, and I'd get jabbed in the stomach as I walk into it. We take short rests to eat from my provisions when I need to, and then Kagami leads the way onward towards what feels like our doom.

We reached the foot of the mountains that night and slept under the branches of a cherry blossom tree.

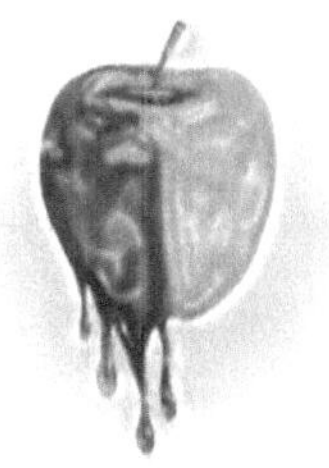

Chapter 40
Trek up the Mountain

When we woke in the morning, I had a meager breakfast from my bag. The trek up the mountain range is even worse than the days before. Kagami does her best to guide me. I find it comforting to feel the fur of her back and tails beneath my fingertips. But my legs burn with every step up the steep trail. I take breaks often and I know Kagami would much rather possess me, and run up the mountain in an instant, but instead she patiently guides me and encourages me to keep going.

Her warm body heat and magic is the only thing that keeps me warm in the cold nights as she curls up on my bedroll and wraps us in an illusion of invisibility, sending our scents elsewhere so we are undetectable. We lay together in the darkness, my sore muscles throbbing.

After three days on the mountain, I'm having trouble breathing when we set out for the day. Every breath feels like a chore and every step feels like I'm moving a mountain rather than walking on one. But I continue on. At around midday Kagami tells me she sees the cottage through the trees. We settle down and rest. We don't know exactly when the miners will show up, and we don't want to be interrupted, so we decide to approach her about an hour after they leave tomorrow for the mines.

We huddled together under a big tree and I sigh with relief when I sit on the cold hard ground. It's still leaning towards summer, but up in the mountains it is much colder, especially at night. I rest my head against the tree and close my eyes against the sunlight streaming through its branches.

Tomorrow, all of Nihon will be safer and nobody will ever know how much danger it was even in. Kagami huffed and rested her head in my lap.

That's okay, we don't need people to know, we just need to do what's right.

But getting praised is so much better!

I laughed and then covered my mouth. Hoping Shirayuki's hearing wasn't good enough to pick up on my blunder.

We sat completely still and I felt warmth surrounding me as Kagami wrapped me in an illusion. I sat there for what felt like hours until I actually wanted to move, which I didn't think would be possible after my trek up a mountainside. Finally, though, Kagami seemed to relax. The warmth of her illusion magic didn't fade, but her breathing steadied, so I shifted to remove my pack and bamboo from my back and grabbed the bed roll from my bag along with some food. I settled back down and ate some dinner before I fell asleep for the night.

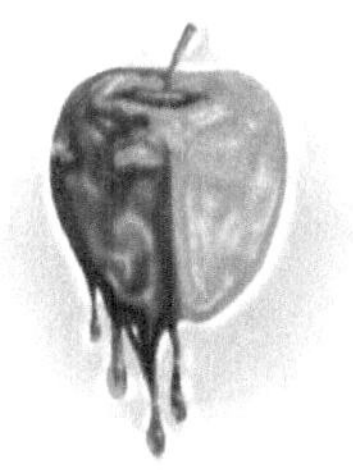

Chapter 41

Burned Alive

The next morning, Kagami woke me up as the first light of dawn was beginning to peak over the horizon.

They just left, she told me, and I stretched and wiped the sleep from my eyes.

Okay let's just confirm. We want to approach as an old woman traveling and selling some wares. We have two kimonos and a hakama that we want to sell her. We offer to help her change, and once we are inside we can wrap her up in the fabric so she can't attack us and then burn her and run away.

Yes. That is the plan.

Okay, we can do this, I told myself more than Kagami. I took the bundle of clothes for Shirayuki out of my bag before packing everything else away.

I snacked on some food while we waited a little longer before approaching the cabin. When I was finished with my breakfast, I stood and slung my bamboo and bag over my shoulder. I held the bundle in one hand and my stick in the other.

You ready? Kagami asked.

Ready.

Alright, now you're a gross old lady, congratulations.

I smiled and bit back a laugh as I walked in the direction of the cabin. Luckily, I was able to follow the path the entire way to it so I didn't need to stumble among the underbrush of the forest to arrive at the cottage. Kagami let me know when to stray off the path and into the clearing the cabin rested in. When I reached the door, I knocked.

Nobody answered. I shifted nervously as I waited.

Try again? Kagami asked.

I knocked again, louder this time. We heard fumbling inside before the door creaked open.

"What is it?" Shirayuki asked with a yawn. We must have woken her.

I didn't speak. I let Kagami's illusion do all the

work, so I heard an old woman's voice say, "I'm traveling to the next city and was looking to sell these clothes for provisions on my journey. Would any of these lovely kimonos interest you?"

"I-" Shirayuki hesitated. "Well, yes, this one is quite lovely,"

"Yes, the finest silks you will find in all of Echigo," the illusion said.

"You smell, I mean it smells familiar, like... magic," she said after a moment.

I bit my lip.

But the illusion around me just cackled, "but of course! Everything I make has a bit of magic in it. I'm a witch!"

I held my breath.

"What kind of witch?" Shirayuki asked, taking a step back.

"The kind that knows a powerful young woman when I see one. The kind that laces magic in the fabric of my clothes that will bring good luck to the wearer, as well as fill you with the confidence to do anything you wish. Those combined will help you accomplish any goal you desire."

I have no idea where Kagami is coming up with

this stuff, but I tried to slowly let out my breath before it became unbearable to hold any longer.

"Well, I suppose it wouldn't hurt, and they are lovely," Shirayuki ventured.

"Oh of course, and they would look so lovely on you. Shall we try one on?"

"Um... okay, sure. Why not"

The door creaked as she opened it wider to allow me to step inside.

Shirayuki led me to a corner where there was a screen for her to change behind. Once she was out of her old kimono I unfolded one of the new ones and held it out for her to slip her arms in. I wrapped it tightly around her middle before I had her step into the hakama and she secured them.

"Oh wow." She breathed. "I've missed having fresh clothes to change into, and they are amazing."

"Come here, let me have a look at you," the illusion said. She stepped in front of me and I placed my hands on her shoulders. "You look like a capable onna-musha[27]," the illusion said.

---

[27] **Onna-musha** /oh-**nah** moo-shah/ - a term referring to a female warrior in feudal Japan.

I let my hands fall along her sleeves and grabbed the long ends that trailed past her fingertips and twirled her around before tying the ends behind her back, pushing her away from me.

Shirayuki grunted as she hit the floor and yelled up at me, "What the heck?"

Kagami brushed past and soon I smelled smoke from her flames.

Shirayuki hissed and cried out as the flames leapt onto her.

I hurried out the door to the cabin, covering my ears against the sounds of her screams and holding my breath against the smell of burning flesh. When I reached the fresh air, I waited for Kagami to join me. I didn't have to wait long. About a minute later Kagami brushed against my leg and let one of her tails rest under my hand so I could use her as a guide as we ran. I held my stick aloft, not wanting it to trip me up, and relied on Kagami's hurried cautions.

"There is a rock, scoot over"

"Step up, there is a log"

"Duck, there is a branch"

When we had run back to our campsite from the night before, we stopped to let me catch my breath.

Kagami let her illusion fall away from me and I felt the cold mountain air seep into me.

"I'm going to keep that fire going for two more hours, then stop it before it catches the cabin on fire." Kagami said.

I just nodded, still gasping for breath.

I held the stitch in my side as I doubled over trying to catch my breath.

Finally, I was able to breathe again, and I sat down, waiting for Kagami to let me know when the fire was out.

After a long wait, she finally said aloud, "Okay, it's out. But I think we should camp here just to be sure before we head back to the village."

"You don't think you killed her?" I asked

"It's hard to tell. She doesn't have a heartbeat to sense. Her new dark essence is still there, lingering, but it could still do that if she were dead. So we just need to wait and see."

I nodded, "Okay we will wait. But I think you should wrap us in invisibility and try to change our scents."

"Okay," she said, and a moment later the warmth of her magic wrapped me in its arms again.

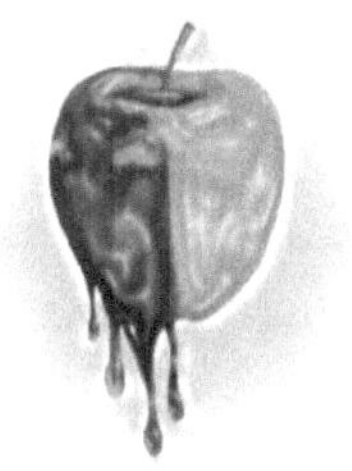

Chapter 42
Plan B

That night, Shirayuki prowled through our campsite. Kagami huddled closer as she came and showed me what she saw.

***

Shirayuki wore the other kimono we had brought and left in the cabin. It was white with red flowers and long flowing sleeves. Tucked into her obi,[28] along with her black hakama, was her sword. Black and red, glinting in the moonlight. Her skin was no longer snow white, but rather an angry red, but as she walked through the trees, the red turned to pink, and soon she was as pale as the moon again.

When she had left, Kagami spoke in my mind.

---

[28] **Obi** /oh-bee/ A long belt tied around the waist on top of the kimono

She's healed completely.

What is she?

Something unstoppable.

No, we just hadn't found the right solution. I thought.

Eventually we fell back asleep.

***

We spent the next morning planning.

If fire didn't kill her, what will? It's the only thing she seemed even remotely afraid of.

I sat in silence, letting Kagami's question bounce around in my head.

What about the sleep powder? That worked.

We want her dead, not asleep.

I know that, but what I mean is what if we get her to eat poison?

How do you plan on doing that? Her diet consists purely of blood.

Magic? I suggested.

Kagami sighed and flopped against my side. We were laying down beneath the big tree within sight of the cabin.

I suppose we could make whatever we need her to eat look irresistible. So she is compelled to try a bite...

Do you think you could do that?

Of course! Kagami said, her indignation flaring up inside me.

Okay, what should we poison? I asked, pulling my pack closer and sitting up.

Digging through the remainder of my food I found an apple.

Would this work? I asked.

Yes, if we found some poison to dip it in. Kagami said.

Have you seen any deadly berries around these woods?

About a half day's walk back, sure.

I grabbed my walking stick and used it to help me stand and turned towards the trail. *Lead on Kagami.*

She brushed past me and led me down the mountain side back the way we came. After a few hours of walking she stopped and told me there was a cluster of bushes a few paces to the left of the trail that were very poisonous.

"Let me guess," I spoke aloud now that we weren't so close to Shirayuki, "you're not going to pick them for me."

"And stain my fur?" Kagami scoffed.

"Right." I grumbled as I poked my stick through the underbrush, trying to find a good place to step.

I tripped over a bush and fell onto the forest floor.

"The good news," Kagami said, laughing, "is that you're right next to the bush now."

I rolled my eyes. "Gee, thanks."

I pulled myself up to a sitting position and winced at the scrapes lining my arms. I pulled a small cloth from my pack and laid it in my lap to collect the berries in, and began stripping the bush I landed next to.

Once I had found all the berries I could, I tied up the corners of the cloth and threw it at Kagami.

"Hey! Watch it!" She wailed in protest

"I don't want them squishing and leaking into all my food," I told her, "so you can hang onto them until I make it back to the trail."

Getting back to Kagami was easier than finding

the berries because the underbrush was crushed from me landing on it.

When I emerged I said, "Okay, is there a stream nearby? Because I need to wash the poison from my hands, and it would probably be a good idea to refill my water. It's getting low."

"There is a stream nearby, but you aren't going to like it." She told me.

"Why?"

"It's pretty far from the trail."

"Great," I groaned.

Her head pressed against my hand before she nudged her snout against it. She was handing me the bundle of berries.

"You don't think I'll squish these and get poison all over me the moment I step off the trail?" I asked, pulling my hand away.

"Good point," she said. "Okay, I'll hide them away in the spirit realm."

"Wait, what? Could you have had my pack in the spirit realm this entire time so I wouldn't have had to carry it?"

"Well...."

"Kagami!"

"What? It's exhausting to go into the spirit realm without an entrance. Not to mention dangerous; any stray spirit could sneak out through my opening, you know that."

I huffed and readjusted my bag on my shoulder.

"Whatever, let's just go."

Kagami clomped her jaw in concentration and a bright light shone in front of me as she created a small opening to the spirit realm and deposited the berries in the opening before closing it up.

"Okay, we will follow the trail up the mountain a little bit, then head to the stream. I think you will have to spend less time off the trail that way."

I thanked her, and we began walking.

When the time came to leave the trail, Kagami guided me as best she could. She let her tail brush against my leg as she picked her way through the bushes and her thoughts sent me a stream of instructions.

There is a ditch up ahead so be careful. There is a log, you are going to need to climb over it, it's fairly small, shouldn't be a problem. Okay, we are about halfway there. Let's go a little to your right to avoid some bushes. Wait, stop, there is a branch sticking up, you need to step over it. There you go Okay we are almost there.

I only tripped two times, and I didn't faceplant once; I was always able to catch myself on a nearby tree. I kept going, branches clawed at my arms and legs as I trampled throughout the underbrush. When we reached the stream, I was very happy to sink to the ground next to it.

I plunged my hands in the water and gasped at the frigid cold that assaulted me.

Still, I kept them submerged and scrubbed.

Kagami finally told me that was good enough when I lost all feeling in my hands.

"Your fingertips are stained, but the poison should be gone."

"Should be?" I asked.

"Probably. Most likely."

"So comforting," I said.

I shuffled upstream a few feet before fumbling with my bag to find my water. Once I got it free, I tried to open it to no avail, my fingers were useless when they were this cold. Kagami sat next to me and curled a tail or two around my hands and they immediately began to warm up. I cried at the painful sensation of my blood pumping back into my fingers, and at the memory of the last time I sat with Kagami trying to get me warm after my water ablutions. Finally, the pain subsided, and I could use my fingers enough to open my water bag. I filled it in the stream, upstream of where I washed my hands so it wasn't tainted, and closed it up.

I put the water away after taking a sip and stood up.

"Okay, let's head back." I said.

"Are you sure? It's getting late. I think we should camp."

"I don't want to have to walk through the underbrush tomorrow, I want to get it over with. We can set up a spot to sleep when we are back on the trail."

"Alright. Fine. Let's get going."

"What are you complaining about?" I asked, following Kagami with my hand on one of her tails.

"I'm not complaining."

"You're being grumpy."

"Okay, I just don't like traipsing through the forest, okay? Branches are getting caught in my beautiful fur, and I am tired of it."

I laughed. "Well, it's no picnic for me either."

"Right, so let's just get it over with so I can get my coat looking amazing again."

I chuckled some more at how vain she was, but said nothing as she carefully guided me back to the trail.

When we reached the trail, I immediately sat down to give my aching legs a break. Kagami told me there was a small open space big enough for the two of us to rest just up the trail, a few feet under a tree. So after a moment I hauled myself back up and trudged over to the tree. Settling down for the night, I pulled out some food to eat. My reserves were getting low, but as long as we headed back in a day or two, I should have enough to last me until we got back home.

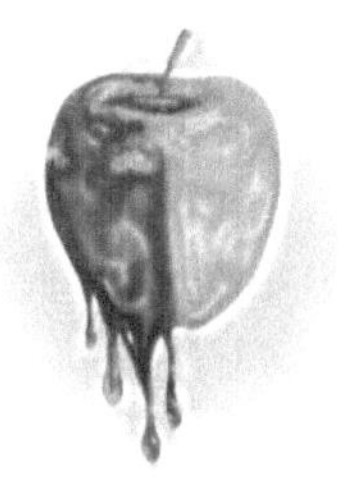

Chapter 43
A Poisoned Apple

We headed out towards the cabin before dawn. The world seemed darker than it did the night before in the hours before the sun peeked over the horizon. As we walked, we talked silently to each other.

How are we going to get her to eat it? I asked.

Same as we got her to try on the dress.

You really think she will fall for an old lady who smells of magic for the second time in three days?

Hmmm.... Maybe you're right. I should change up the illusion... Perhaps you should be injured.

I don't want to bleed in front of her. My foot caught on a loose rock and I almost tripped.

Just like a limp or something. Kagami says, brushing away my concern.

I still don't think she will fall for it again.

That's why it's called magic, Yumi. It takes all your common sense and throws it out the window. That apple will look irresistible to her; she will be dying to take a bite. Quite literally, in fact.

I sighed. I suppose we don't have much of an option except leaving it out in hopes she would find it, but then anyone could eat it.

Fine, we will try it your way again.

Hey, my way worked just fine. It's not my fault she can heal faster than I could burn her.

We were silent for a while, lost in thoughts and focusing on the trail ahead. The sun began streaming light across my vision and as it rose higher.

Finally I asked, *How much longer?*

We are almost there, maybe an hour to the clearing we stayed in that's in sight of the cottage.

So we walked on, Kagami by my side and my stick out in front of me searching for obstacles.

When we arrived at the clearing an hour later. Kagami asked me to get the apple out while she retrieved the berries from the spirit realm. I dug through my bag as a blinding flash assaulted my eyes before it dimmed. When I finally felt the smooth sphere I pulled it out.

Here, I said.

Hmmm, earth and nature isn't my specialty, and it would be ideal to not get your hands covered in poison again when you have to touch the apple.

Are you saying this isn't going to work?

No I'm saying give me a second. This requires focus.

I pursed my lips and kept my thoughts to myself.

The air around Kagami warmed and an orange glow surrounded her in a haze. I couldn't see exactly what she was doing but I imagined she was trying to merge the two fruits.

Finally the glow faded and Kagami panted as she flopped onto the dirt with a thud.

Are you okay!? I said, barely remembering to remain quiet and only speak in my mind.

Yes, I'm just exhausted.

I didn't know you could get exhausted.

Well earth isn't my thing, so it took a lot of magic, and I still only did it half way. If you wanted me to burn the whole world down, I could do that no problem and still have fire left.

Yeah, we aren't doing that.

Whatever you say.

So, what do you mean by halfway?

You gave me a white apple. I tried to infuse the red poisonous berries into it, but ran out of energy halfway, so now you have a half red, half white apple. The red side is poisonous, the white is just a normal apple.

And I'm okay to touch it? I asked

Yes, it shouldn't leave a residue of poison because the apple peel is tougher than the berries.

I reached out and found the apple in the space between us. It felt the same as before, just a regular apple. I gently tossed it in the air and caught it.

Careful, Kagami chided, *don't want it exploding poisonous goop all over you if you don't catch it.*

Whatever, I rolled my eyes, setting the apple neatly on my lap.

After a while Kagami said, *Okay, you ready?*

Yes but do you have enough energy?

Yes. I'm just going to stay here and wrap you in an illusion, I'm going to project what is happening too, so that way you know which side of the apple we want her to eat.

Okay, I grumbled

Aww, the poor blind girl will be able to see. Kagami teased.

I just... it's disorienting, and I kind of like the way that I am. I don't need to be fixed.

Well, for the next half hour you need to be able to see.

Let's just get this over with.

I stood and faced the direction of the cottage as the world around me shifted from light and dark fuzzy patches to crystal clear color. Trees morphed from the shadows and reached high into the sky. The dark green bushes that clustered around them had prickly thorns that said 'don't step on me.' The green grass of the clearing where we sat. It all came into view.

I wavered, dizziness washing over me as I adjusted to this new image in my mind. I looked down to see that I was wearing an old, tattered kimono that was dark in color. My hands were wrinkled with age, and I had a basket filled with apples. I clutched the half poisonous apple in my other hand and began walking toward the cabin that I could just make out the shape of between the trees at the edge of the clearing.

I carefully tread along the path, watching my steps as I walked. It was weird seeing the ground as I walked, it seemed too close to me. I felt like with every step I might fall over. However, by the time I'd reached the cottage I was getting a little more used to navigating the world around me.

The cottage was small, wooden, and a little run down. There were patches of the walls and roof that had been boarded up, and some of the shutters looked broken. But overall, it looked like a nice, quiet place to live. I walked up onto the porch and knocked on the door. I heard Shirayuki inside as she made her way to the door. When it opened, I tried my best to keep my composure.

"I am trying to lighten my load for my journey, my arms can't hardly hold this basket of apples. Would you like to take some?" I heard my illusioned voice say. It wasn't the same as last time, it sounded more frail and unassuming. I held out the apple with its half poisoned side angled towards her.

Shirayuki furrowed her brow, "I'm sorry, I don't like apples."

She began to close the door when my illusion said, "Are you sure?"

Suddenly I felt the strongest desire to eat the apple. It looked like it would be the most delicious thing on the planet. I knew that if I ate that apple, I wouldn't be hungry ever again. The door opened wider and I was vaguely aware of Shirayuki's hand reaching out to the apple.

"No," she said, pulling her hand away, "I shouldn't have even opened the door, I'm sorry."

"What if we just split it. I don't imagine you get much fruit up here in the mountains besides berries. Care to let an old woman rest and share an apple? I'll eat the white cheek and you can have the red cheek.

Shirayuki licked her lips. As another wave of desire washed over us. I needed that apple. If I didn't have it, I might as well let Shirayuki drain me of my blood right here and now. The sun glinted off its shiny dome, and I almost shoved it in my mouth right then.

My hand trembled as I held it out to Shirayuki. It was the last thing I wanted to do, but I kept chanting in my head. *You can't eat it, it's poisonous. You can't eat it, it's poisonous.*

I gritted my teeth to stop myself from taking a

bite out of the apple.

"Well, okay, just this one. Let me get a knife," she left the door wide open and I walked into the small interior. There was a staircase in the back of the room leading upstairs to where they would sleep, I assumed. They had a small kitchen and a long low table occupied most of the middle of the room. I sat on the ground by the table, and placed the apple on the table with great difficulty. Shirayuki came back, and her kimono sleeves fluttered around her as she settled next to me. She cut the apple in half and handed me the white side. Holding the red in her hand, watching me carefully.

I took the apple and bit into it moaning with delight at the delicious flavor that was promised. I chewed and swallowed and took another bite.

Then Shirayuki finally gave in and took a huge bite of her half. She didn't chew it though, she tried to swallow it whole and it got lodged in her throat. She began gasping and coughing. She reached out to me but I scrambled back in fear. Her skin, already pale, drained of what little color was left and with a few more coughs, she collapsed on the floor, convulsing. I sat there and watched until she became still.

Then it finally hit me.

I killed her. I killed Kenshin's daughter, I killed Kagekatsu's little sister. I killed one of my only friends.

The horror of what I'd done bubbled up inside me and tears poured out of me as my body was wracked with sobs. I knew, I knew that it was the only way, that she wasn't Shirayuki anymore, but still, seeing her limp before me, her lifeless eyes, pleading up at me to help her. And I just sat there and watched. That image was burned into my memory. I scrambled father away from her before I collapsed in a heap and let myself fall apart. I cried for what felt like hours.

Eventually, the illusion of the old woman fell away from me and I was left as a young 17 year old girl again. My kimono was covered in dirt from my travels and my hair was falling out of its ponytail, half covering my face. I could still see, but I knew Kagami was weak from merging the apple and the berries. I closed my eyes and focused on her energy inside me and applied pressure. I pushed and pushed until I forced her out of my mind. I could find my way back to her on my own, but right now I wanted to be alone. And I wanted the sight of Shirayuki's dead form out of my head.

I curled up and cried until I couldn't cry anymore. I vaguely remember Kagami's presence trying to press into my mind, trying to fill the growing void in my soul, but I pushed her away. She needed to rest for the journey home. And I needed to be alone.

Finally, when the light coming in through the open door dimmed, I heard a faint whistling sound. I sat up slowly, the world listing around me and I listened more closely. Someone was coming, or maybe multiple people, as more harmonies reached my ears.

The miners! I thought.

I scrambled to my feet and hurried out the door. I ran around to the back of the cottage and crouched down behind it. I didn't know how close they were and if they could see the cottage or not. I didn't want to risk them seeing me, and if they took the same trail I did, I might bump into them when they turned towards the cabin. I'd wait here for them to settle into bed, then I'd sneak back to Kagami.

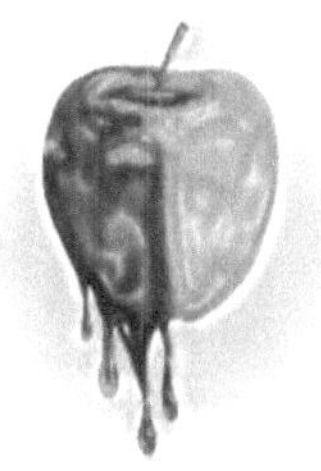

Chapter 44
No Forever with Humans

I sank further to the ground, sat with my back to the wall, and hugged my knees trying, to be as small as possible.

The whistling got louder and louder until one of the miners called out: "Shirayuki!"

The whistling stopped and the air was filled with low murmurs and gasps as they all saw what I had done.

After a moment a gruff voice said, "I can't find her heartbeat. She's so cold, she's been dead for a while."

If only he knew just how long she's been without a heart, I thought bitterly.

The miners decided to lay her in her bed for the night, and tomorrow they would build her a place to rest.

I waited until I couldn't hear them anymore, aside from the soft sound of them snoring upstairs.

I straightened and quietly made my way around the house and towards the path that would lead me to Kagami. I walked carefully and slowly through the darkness from memory, and finally, I made it back to the clearing.

"Kagami?" I called.

A faint glow flickered off to my right and I hurried over to her.

"You pushed me away," she said weakly.

"You needed your strength more than I did." I said running my hands along her matted fur.

"I thought we were going to be together forever."

I chuckled, swiping away a tear that I didn't think I had any left of.

"You know there is no forever with humans."

She climbed onto my lap and collapsed into me, almost knocking me over.

"A fox can dream," she said contentedly and drifted off to sleep.

Carefully, I pulled my bag and bamboo from my back, grabbed my blanket from it and laid down on it and fell asleep.

This time, there was no warmth of her illusion magic wrapped around me. We had nothing to hide from anymore.

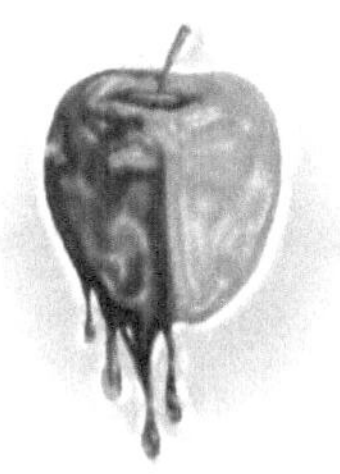

Chapter 45

A Victorious Return

We stayed in the clearing for two days. We wanted to watch the cottage and make sure Shirayuki was in fact dead, and we also needed to let Kagami rest after she overused magic of which she had very little connection to.

We sat and rested, chatting for the whole day about what our future could look like without the threat of Shirayuki looming over us anymore. I joked that maybe Kagekatsu might finally ask me to marry him and Kagami said she was surprised he hadn't already.

"For someone as brave as him on the battlefield, he is a big coward," she said.

I laughed. It felt good to be just the two of us again.

When night was about to fall, Kagami was doing better, so she searched for Shirayuki and told me what she saw. The miners had made a place for her to lay out in front of their cottage. She laid there as if taking a nap, she looked peaceful. They had even combed her hair. One of them was chipping away at a stone, and when he was finally done, they rested it at the foot of the bed she laid on. It said:

"Here lies Shirayuki, the most beautiful woman in Nihon."

The next day, the miners began building a structure around Shirayuki's body to shield it from the elements.

*****

"They aren't going to bury her?" I asked incredulously.

"Apparently not," Kagami said. She sounded just as disturbed as I was. "They think she is too beautiful to hide away in the earth. This way they can still see her everyday. It's quite gross."

I shuddered at the thought of Shirayuki's spirit not being laid to rest properly and becoming a demon.

"To be fair, she was essentially already a

demon" Kagami said, reading my thoughts. "Besides, you can handle that sort of demon."

That was true. Spirit realm monsters were easy.

***

We set out for home around midday, not wanting to stay longer than we had to now that Kagami was back at full strength again. I shouldered my pack and grabbed my walking stick.

"Let's head home, Kagami," I said.

***

The journey back was uneventful, and when we finally made it back to the pagoda, I was met with a warm welcome. All the maids and guards came to greet me and asked where I had been. And I told them everything over a nice hot beef pot.

They cheered when I confirmed that Shirayuki was dead, though some grumbled that it was a pity that this was the only way.

I agreed.

Finally, I asked the question that had been burning in my mind. "Where's Kagekatsu?"

"He left for the front. I'm sure he will be back in a few weeks time. He wanted to wait for your return, he was worried sick, but..." Koga trailed off.

I just nodded, "That's good. We need to show that despite the tragedies in the Uesugi household, we are still strong."

The room filled with silence. Kagami nudged my hand with her head so I pet her.

He will be back, she said in my mind.

I smiled down at her, *I know.*

A maid broke the silence and asked if I wanted her to fill a warm bath.

"That would be amazing!" I said.

And the room erupted in laughter as they took in my filthy appearance from weeks out in the woods.

***

After relaxing in the warm bath and scrubbing my guilt and dirt off with a vengeance, I collapsed into my own bed and fell straight to sleep with Kagami curled up beside me.

I could end the story here. I could pretend that we all lived happily ever after. Kagekatsu returned from the front to scoop me in his arms and ask for my hand in marriage. A year later, my parents came for the wedding celebration, beaming with joy. The world was safe. It didn't matter if Kagekatsu was able to hold off Nobunaga's army or not. Nothing could be worse than what we already had lived through. But you know the story doesn't end here. Shirayuki doesn't stay dead.

Part 3

Shirayuki's Rebirth

10 Years later

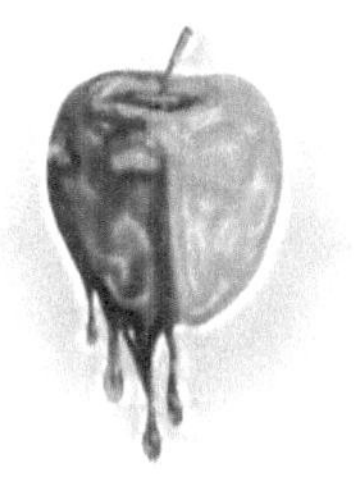

Chapter 46
A Wedding Invitation

I'm walking the halls of the pagoda, Kagami at my side, listening for the sounds of giggling.

She's up ahead in the training room.

I smiled. No one could hide from Kagami and me. I burst through the training room door and pointed straight ahead.

"I found you!" I shouted triumphantly.

A shriek of surprise greeted my ears.

"No fair! Kagami told you! Didn't she?" My little girl pouted. But she still barreled into my legs. I picked her up and gave her a big hug.

"Oh it's okay, I'll tell you where your older brother is hiding."

"Really!?"

I whispered in her ear and she wriggled to get down, I set her on her feet and listened to the soft patter of her feet as they ran away to find her brother hiding in the kitchen.

"Yumi!" Kagekatsu called out to me in a worried voice.

"I'm in here!" I called, re-emerging into the hallways and knocking into him.

He caught me before I could fall.

"Yumi, when was the last time Kagami checked on Shirayuki?" His voice trembled in fear.

I turned to Kagami.

"I- I- it's been so long I haven't been checking as frequently. It's been months, maybe a year." Kagami spoke aloud to Kagekatsu.

"Why?" I asked.

"Can you just check her, please? Then I'll explain."

Kagami went quiet for a second before she gasped, "She's not there!'

"What?" I spoke at the same time as Kagekatsu said, "So it's true,"

His legs buckled and he caught himself on the

wall. His voice was barely a whisper when he spoke, "Show me Kagami, please."

***

The scene appeared in my mind. The little cottage nestled in the wood with a small structure outside it. The structure was where Shirayuki used to lay with a plaque that said: "Here lies Shirayuki, the most beautiful woman in Nihon." But as Kagami's sight came closer to the structure, you could see that Shirayuki's body was gone. Not even the table she laid on was there.

***

The scene disappeared. I blinked.

"What happened?" I whispered.

"I don't know," Kagami said bitterly.

"We got an invitation to go to her wedding." Kagekatsu thrust a scroll into my hand, and I clutched it.

"WHAT?" I demanded.

"Yeah, Hideyoshi succeeded Nobunaga after his death. That's who she is marrying."

"But... he's, both her fathers' greatest enemy. He stands for everything she despises."

"I think she realized she couldn't come back and claim this clan, so she decided to rule another." Kagekatsu said.

"And she invited us to the wedding?" I asked.

"She has to be taunting us."

"Obviously," Kagami muttered.

"What are we going to do?"

"Eat and get drunk at the happy couple's expense?" Kagami suggested.

I glared down at her.

"Is that a no?"

I rolled my eyes, "It's a no," I said.

"Well," Kagekatsu said. "What if we went? She wouldn't want to ruin her own wedding. I don't think she would make a scene, and we can try and assess the situation. Maybe she's healed."

His voice was quiet as he said the last part.

I placed my hand on his arm. He was one of the first ones to suggest that killing Shirayuki was the only way. That she couldn't be healed. But he must have secretly wished there was a way to save his adopted sister; that's why he let me try.

"Okay, we will go. Besides, I want Kagami to

read her. The only way to do that is to get close to her. She can smell magic, but at her wedding maybe she won't be as on guard with all the guests tempting her with a feast. Or maybe you're right, and she's cured." I added, for Kagekatsu's benefit, though I didn't even want to hope that this was true.

Chapter 47
Revenge

When it came time to travel to the wedding, we set off. Kagami appeared as a young woman traveling with us so as to blend in as we traveled through the cities. When we finally reached the Owari[29] province, everyone was tense. We arrived in the city the night before the wedding and stayed at an inn.

We didn't sleep much that night. We all laid awake wondering what tomorrow would bring. A mix of guilt and dread crept into my heart at the thought of facing Shirayuki again after what I'd done. How I just sat there and watched as she slowly died. I wiped a tear from my cheek, and tried to think of anything else. That seemed an impossible feat though, as the guilt just came crashing over me

---

[29] **Owari** /oh-**wah**-ree/ - an old province in Nihon (Japan) where Oda Nobunaga lived.

again and again, until I finally fell into a restless sleep plagued with nightmares of the past.

***

In the morning, I was nauseous from my nerves. I did not want to go to this wedding. I knew it was a terrible idea. But instead, I got dressed in my nicest kimono, ate as much breakfast as my stomach could handle, and slung my bamboo stick across my back and secured my wooden box around my waist before draping my rosary over my head. This made me feel better. But only a little.

I should have known something was wrong when Kagami couldn't cross the threshold.

"It's like there are wards," she complained. "It's fine though, you guys go. I'll keep watch out here.

Reluctantly we entered the wedding without her and mingled with the crowd.

We didn't speak of how we knew Shirayuki, just that she was an old friend, as we waited for her and her soon to be husband to arrive.

When they did, a hush fell over the noisy crowd as they addressed the masses.

"As most of you all know," Hideyoshi said in a booming voice, "I rescued Shirayuki from a fate far worse than death and years of torment. She was kept captive by her own family when she was young, and finally escaping, she found refuge in the mountains with some kindly miners who offered her shelter and food. But her family couldn't stand the thought that she had slipped through their grasp. And so they hunted her down and killed her!" A collective gasp echoed through the crowd.

"Poisoned her with an apple, she was left for dead in an eternal endless sleep. The miners thought she was too young, too pure to be put away in the dirt and laid her in a coffin of glass in the woods. That's where I found her. The moment I laid eyes on her I knew I was in love. I didn't want to leave her side. I begged the miners that I should have her. That I would give anything to bring her home with me. Eventually they relented, and I picked her up and began carrying her home. Only when I moved her did she cough up the poisonous apple and was revived from her eternal sleep! I immediately asked her to marry me, of which she accepted, and we made for home at once!"

Cheers arose from the crowd as they clapped and celebrated their new Daimyō's wife.

"So that's how she's alive again," Kagekatsu murmured.

Yumi, get out now! Kagami spoke in my mind,

You need to leave NOW!

I turned to Kagekatsu and slipped my arm through his pulling him to the back of the crowd.

"We need to leave, something's not right," I whispered.

Before he could respond, Hideyoshi's voice called out again to the crowd.

"Which is why as my wedding gift to you, my dear Shirayuki, I give you," he paused for dramatic effect, "revenge."

I furrowed my brow and began trying to push my way out of the middle of the crowd.

"Yumi!" Shirayuki called out in a singsong voice, "Where are you going?"

A hush fell over the crowd and I felt a million eyes on me as the crowd shifted around me and Kagekatsu.

"You don't want to miss my wedding do you? We were just getting to the good part"

I turned to face her, guilt eating away at my insides. Guilt for killing her, guilt for not succeeding, and fear of what was to come made my hand tremble.

I heard Kagekatsu draw his sword and many

others being drawn.

Shirayuki tsks, "You know you're completely outmatched brother, and that's if it was only me. Now add my new royal guards, well. You don't stand a chance."

"I won't let you touch her," he growled.

"Where was this fierce loyalty when everyone wanted me dead? Do you care so little for your little sister? "

"You know that was different, you were out of control."

Shirayuki dropped her voice so only we could hear.

"And now?" She asked, "Look at me standing in a room full of blood and not even bothered. I always had control. You just never gave me a chance."

"Murdering innocent people at your father's funeral. You call that control?" I hissed.

"Shh, of course!" she said in a calm voice. "I needed you to know who you were dealing with."

I scoffed.

Yumi! I still can't enter the building! Someone did put wards up around it!

What?

We left Kagami outside the wedding to read Shirayuki and assess the situation from there, but it turns out Shirayuki figured out how to block all spirits from entering her home. She must have found a powerful shaman to perform the spell.

I'm sorry, I can't help you! You need to get out so I can protect you!

Dread filled me up, hardened, and dropped to the pit of my stomach. I felt sick.

"Now, Kagekatsu, I believe I told you this doesn't have anything to do with you." Shirayuki said. Lightning fast Kagekatsu was pulled from my side and he thudded to the ground groaning.

"Restrain him," Shirayuki commanded.

Many footsteps marched forward and dragged my dazed husband away into the crowd.

"What do you want, Shirayuki?" I demanded.

"I want you to suffer," she said, snapping her fingers.

More footsteps came and I heard them dump something on the ground. It collided with the floor and skidded to my feet.

Searing hot pain burned through me, and I

leapt back from the rock that had landed on my foot.

"Now dance," Shirayuki said.

"What?"

"Take off your socks and dance on the hot coals until I say you can stop or else Kagekatsu dies."

"Yumi don't!" I heard Kagekatsu yell from the crowd behind me.

But I couldn't let him pay for my sins. Kagami couldn't come in and provide a distraction for escape. This was the only way.

I slipped off my socks and stepped forward onto the hot coals that were spread out on the ground before me and started to dance.

Chapter 48
Death's Door

Yumi no!

"Yumi!"

Pain shot through my feet and I screamed, tears pouring down my face, but I didn't stop for fear they would kill Kagekatsu. I couldn't let my children become orphans. If he could survive this through my sacrifice, then at least they would have their father to raise them.

I couldn't hear anything above the pain in my feet and my own cries of pain. I always thought that nothing could offer worse suffering than starving for a hundred days all just to have freezing water dumped on me repeatedly until I lost consciousness. But this? This was worse. A thousand times worse.

Finally, when I couldn't take it anymore, I collapsed onto the ground amidst the coals and screamed as I was burned all along my side. I tried to jerk away but there was no way I could escape the coals on my own in my state. All I was conscious of was pain.

Hands grabbed me and dragged me off the hot coals and through the crowd. The heat lessened, but it still burned. My feet felt like they were on fire and I couldn't seem to stop screaming.

Finally, I was thrust onto the ground and someone landed on top of me.

Kagekatsu scrambled off and started talking a mile a minute, but I didn't understand anything he said. I just screamed from pain that wouldn't stop.

As I laid there writhing in pain, I had the thought that this was how I was going to die.

Then suddenly, I felt relief.

My feet still throbbed with pain, but it was bearable.

I blinked and swiped away my tears with my hand that didn't land on the coals. My whole side burned, but it was manageable, barely.

Yumi! Yumi!

"What Kagami?" I muttered aloud, exhausted.

"Oh, thank goodness you're okay." Kagekatsu brushed a tear off my cheek.

"What happened?"

"When you collapsed they dragged us out. I ran to get a bucket of water. That's why your feet feel a little better."

I nodded. I couldn't feel my feet aside from the throbbing, but it made sense if they were submerged in water.

"I'm so sorry I couldn't protect you," he said. He rested his head on my arm as he clutched my uninjured hand.

"Don't be. There wasn't anything you could have done. We are no match for her." My words slurred together.

"Kagekatsu, I think she's dying," Kagami said.

Sobs racked through his body as he whispered, "No you can't die!"

"You're right,' I managed. "I can't. Shirayuki played the long game, but so can I."

"What are you talking about Yumi?" Kagekatsu asked.

"Kagami, you said you wanted to be with me forever. You can make me live forever."

"Yumi, at this point, the only thing that would save you is if I possessed you and you took on my fire abilities to be able to withstand your injuries."

"I know. Just do it. We will live forever like Shirayuki, and one day we will find a way to kill her."

"I- I can't just- no!" Kagami said.

Kagekatsu spoke up in a quiet voice, "Do it. Kagami, it's the only way."

"You realize you'd be married to both of us then right?"

"Like that wasn't the case already." Kagekatsu forced out a laugh.

And finally, Kagami relented, just as I lost consciousness.

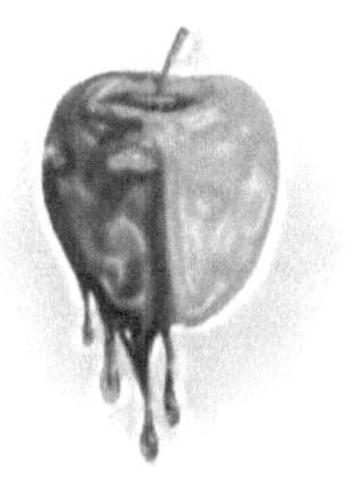

Chapter 49
Yugami

Being possessed by a Kitsune is the exact opposite feeling of the dead possessing you. Instead of feeling a deep cold wrap around your soul, warmth fills you up inside.

I don't know how long I was unconscious, fighting for a balance between my consciousness and hers, but eventually we compromised.

When I opened my eyes, the light was tinged with red. But I still couldn't see any better than I had when I passed out. I felt full of energy, like I could run up a mountain and back and be ready to do it again. But most of all, I felt like me.

You are, Kagami said. *For the most part*

I sat up and ran my hand through my hair to find my hand blocked by... fuzzy ears? I began to panic. I felt the ears and sure enough they were foxes ears sticking out of the top of my head. I ran my hands along my arms but they still felt normal and my hands were hands not paws. I froze as a thought occurred to me. *Did I have a tail?*

I reached behind me and felt the familiar touch of Kagami's coat.

You have 7 tails, actually, Kagami told me.

I groaned and buried my face in my hands.

You wouldn't let me give you sight, so I had to give you some other traits. It needed to balance out. We are quite beautiful though.

"How would you know?" I grumbled "You're blind now remember?"

Actually, I have my own way of seeing. Still pretty frustrating that you wouldn't let me fix you though.

The door slid open, and I heard Kagekatsu gasp in surprise, "Yumi you're awake!"

I yelped in surprise trying to hide my ears, throwing my hands over my head.

His footsteps faltered.

"It is you? Right?" He sounded so uncertain.

"Yes it's me," I said quietly.

"And me!" A voice that was slightly higher pitched than my own leapt from my lips.

I scowled. I didn't realize she could do that.

Oh, we can do many things, Kagami whispered in my head.

"Well, that's good. I think." The bedroll shifted as he sat down next to me.

I still didn't look in his direction but he slowly reached out and put my hands down in my lap and pulled my chin to face him.

Tears sprang to my eyes.

"There's Yumi," he said and gently kissed my forehead.

I hugged him, letting my grief wash me away until finally I could breathe again.

"What have I done?" I said.

"You did what you had to do. Together you and Kagami will wait out Shirayuki, watch her, and find her weakness. When the moment is right you will kill her. For good this time."

I closed my eyes. I knew that's what I had to do.

"But what about you and the children?"

"We will help for as long as we can."

I took a deep breath to steady myself.

Okay. We can do this, I thought.

That's the spirit! Kagami chimed in. *This will be fun!*

To be continued...

Glossary

Ablution /ah-**bloo**-shon/ Purification method involving dumping cold water on the subject repeatedly.

Daimyō /**dah**-ee-mee-oh/ feudal lords who acted as vessels of the Shogun in their province. Typically, they were given free reign of their province. In the time period of this book the daimyōs were fighting to unite all of Japan under one rule, and the result of the war led to the Edo period with all of Japan under a single families rule.

Echigo /**ee**-chi-go/ -an old providence in Nihon where the Uesugi clan where located. (Japan)

Gehobako /ge-**ho**-ba-ko/ Small wooden box containing figurines and charms used in shamanic rituals.

Geta /**geh**-tah/ Traditional japanese footwear resembling flip flops with two big blocky "teeth" on the bottom. A traditional Japanese wooden clog that is worn outdoors, with a thong that passes between the first two toes and with two transverse supports on the bottom of the soles.

Hakama /ha-**kah**-mah/ a type of traditional Japanese clothing. Loose trousers with many pleats in the front, worn over the kimono. Frequently worn by samurai.

Hakkyu-go Batsujonogi /ha-**kyu** go **ba**-su-joh-noh-gee/ the act of purifying the home after the body is removed from where the funeral took place. Priests will offer prayers and offerings to the gods to cleanse the home now that the body has been moved. The funeral alter is removed and a new alter is set up inside the home in remembrance of the deceased.

Itako /**ee**-ta-koh/ Blind women trained to be spiritual medians.
Kawamura, Kunimitsu. <u>"The Life of a Shamaness: Scenes from the Shamanism of Northeastern Japan"</u>. *Kokugakuin.*

Kai /**kai**/ an old providence in Nihon where the Takeda clan was located. (Japan)

Kami /**kah**-mee/ revered deities and spirits in the shinto religion, interconnected with nature and the natural world.

Kamituke /**kah**-mee-too-keh/ a ritual performed during an Itako's final ceremony to determine which deity will claim their as their 'bride' and be their patron granting them power to commune with the spiritual realm. Kawamura, Kunimitsu. *"The Life of a Shamaness: Scenes from the Shamanism of Northeastern Japan"*. *Kokugakuin*.

Katana /**kah**-tah-na/ a long, curved single-edged sword traditionally used by Japanese samurai.

Kimono /**kee**-moh-no/ Traditional Japanese garment, a loose, wide-sleeved robe, fastened at the waist with a wide sash, (see Obi) characteristic of medieval Japanese wear

Kitsune /**kit**-soo-neh/ Term used in Japanese folklore that refers to foxes with supernatural abilities. These are spiritual beings with shapeshifting abilities along with using intricate illusions. Also known as demons who are known for seducing men and devouring their souls.

Kuchiyose /koo-**chee**-yo-seh / - Literally translated to 'drawing in to speak' it refers to the practice of allowing spirits to possess one's body and speak through it.

Kudoki /koo-**doh**-kee/ - Songs used in shamanic and shinto rituals.

Mizugori /mee-zoo-**goh**-ree/ cold water ablutions for the purpose of purifying the individual before or during an important event.

Necromancer /neh-**kroh**-man-ser/ a person who uses shamanic rituals and magic to reanimate dead people or to foretell the future by communicating with them.

Nihon /**nee**-hon/ Japan Nihonjin -japanese. The Japanese word for Japan.

Obi /oh-bee/ A long belt tied around the waist on top of the kimono

Onna-musha /oh-**nah** moo-shah/ - a term referring to a female warrior in feudal Japan.

Owari /oh-**wah**-ree/- an old providence in Nihon where Oda Nobunaga and Hideyoshi Toyotomi lived (Japan)

Saké /**sah**-keh/ Alcoholic beverage, usually a wine made from rice.

Setta /**seh**-tah/ traditional Japanese footwear resembling flip flops, with a smooth sole, more suitable for samurai and others to wear who needed to have better balance than the geta would provide.

Seppuku /seh-**puu**-kuu/ the honorable method of taking one's own life practiced by samurai in feudal Japan. Usually done by warriors who were defeated in battle, or to avoid the dishonor of falling into enemy hands. This is done by plunging a short sword into the left side of the abdomen, drawing the blade laterally across to the right, and then turn it upward. Being an extremely slow and painful means of suicide it was viewed as a way for the samurai to demonstrate courage, resolve, and self control to inflict it on ones self.

See www.britanica.com/topic/suppuku

Shaman /**shaa**-men/ a person who acts as intermediary between the natural and supernatural worlds, using magic to cure illness, foretell the future, control spiritual forces, etc.

Shogunate /**sho**-gun-ate/ a form of government in feudal Japan, in which power was held by the Shogun, a military dictator. In this time period he had daimyo ruling various provinces. These three main daimyo (Nobunaga, Kenshin, and Shingen) were essentially giving free reign over their provinces and fought to unite all of Japan under one of their rules, overthrowing the current shogun and replacing them.

Tessen /**teh**-sen/Japanese war fan. Or 'iron fan' used as a weapon or for signaling.

Character guide

Atagi Tsubu /**ah**-tah-gee **tsoo**-boo/ Guard

Enya Sadaharu /**ehn**-yah sah-**dah**-ha-roo/ Guard

Fujioka Gin /foo-**gee**-oh-kah **gin**/ Guard

Hideyoshi Toyotomi /hee-**dee**-yo-shee too-yo-**toh**-mee/ Successor to Nobunaga March 17 1537- Sept 18 1598

*Fictionally Shirayuki's Husband in part 3 Shirayuki's rebirth.

Honjou Morosuke /**hon**-joh mo-**roh**-soo-keh/ Guard

Kagami /kah-**gah**-mee/ Means mirror- Kitsune(see glossary for Kitsune) Favored element: Fire. *Completely fictional.

Koga Tomotame /**koh**-gah to-mo-**tah**-meh/ Captain of the guards at the Castle in Echigo.

Master Fujimori /foo-gee-**moh**-ree/ -necromancer- Trains Yumi. *Completely fictional

Nakamikado Tame /nah-ka-mee-**ka**-doh **tah**-meh/ Guard

Oda Nobunaga /**oh**-dah no-boo-**nah**-gah/ Rival to

the west Daimyo of Owari June23 1534 - 21 June 1582

Shirayuki /**shee**-rah-yoo-kee/ means snow white. Daughter of Shingen, adopted after his death by Kenshin. *Completely fictional.

Takeda Shingen /**tah**-keh-dah **shee**-n-gehn/ Tiger of Kai- Daimyo - December 1 1521 -May 13 1573 (*fictionally Shirayuki's father) Kenshin's Rival in the south. Historically he had 11 children

Tokiwa /**to**-kee-wah/ everlasting -Kagami's sister - Controls time -Kitsune *Completely Fictional

Tsugaru /soo-**gah**-roo/ Guard.

Tsukuyomi /soo-ko-**yo**-mee/ God of the moon- *Yumi "married" him at the end of her Itako ceremony.

Uesugi Kagekatsu /**yoo**-eh-seh-gee kah-geh-**kah**-tsoo/ First adopted son of Kenshin and nephew by blood. Historically he is younger than Kagetora but adopted first, and he married one of Shingen's daughters 1555-1623

*Fictionally he marries Yumi

Uesugi Kagetora /**yoo**-eh-seh-gee kah-geh-**toh**-rah/ Second adopted son of Kenshin 1552-April 19 1579 committed seppuku after being defeated by Kagekatsu.

Uesugi Kenshin /**yoo**-eh-seh-gee **kehn**-shen/ Dragon of Itako- Daimyō, February 18 1530 - April 19th 1578 Adopts Kagekatsu and Kagetora (*and fictional Shirayuki.)

When Shingen died he cried and said "I have lost my good rival. We won't have a hero like that again!" ref: (Sato, hiroaki (1995) legends of the samurai overlook duckworth isbn 9781590207307)

Death poem reference: (Suzuki, Daisetsu Teitaro (1993) Zen and Japanese Culture. Princeton. Isbn 9780691017709)

Ujie Yasutoshi /**oo**-gee ya-soo-**toh**-shee/ Guard.

Urakami Mitsu /oo-rah-**ka**-mee **mee**-tsoo/ Maid Servant.

Yumi /**yoo**-mee/ means Beauty- Itako (see glossary for Itako.) *Completely fictional.

Acknowledgements

First and foremost, I would like to acknowledge my Father in Heaven, without His help none of this would have been possible. From the inspiration to write, the support from on high to finish and the strength to continue even when times are tough. I know I can weather any storm and accomplish anything with His love and support behind me.

I also want to put in an honorable mention here to all of the young Christian authors who I follow and support on social media. You have been amazing examples to me of how to be an disciple of Christ and acknowledging his hand in my life and not being worried about shouting it out to the world. It was an important lesson I should have learned years ago, but your example gave me the push I needed, so thank you.

Next, I must say a huge thank you to my team of beta readers and editors. Hollie, Julia, and Leesa you are amazing and made this story so much better than I could have on my own. Thank you for your invaluable help and encouragement through this process. It really is only as good as it is because of you, you're amazing.

And of course, I cannot forget to mention Rhonda who drew the chapter heading art. She did a phenomenal job with the prompt I gave her and drew that apple so much better than I could have. You're a good person to have around Rhonda.

Lastly but certainly not the least. I want to thank my family for putting up with me and supporting me in this endeavor through the long hours of writing, audio recording, editing, and drawing so I could finish this book. I am so grateful for your patience and support; it means the world to me that you believe in these stories as much as I do.

About the Author

V. Kay Perks is a Christian author specializing in fractured fairy tales and fantasy. She has a Post-Graduate Certificate in Creative Writing, which is what she likes to do when she's not hanging out with her favorite people (her husband and children). Born and raised in Lancaster, California, she now lives with her husband and kids in Salt Lake City, UT. Her favorite activities include sewing stuffed animals, drawing, reading, and walking to the local library. She always tries to be up on current events at the library and loves getting involved in all their reading programs.

If you would like to see more of her, you can check out her social media accounts here!

She is on Instagram, Facebook, and TikTok @V.kayperks

Want some awesome merch? We got that too!

Check out V. Kay Perks own store!

Books with Perks!

Bringing you LIT-erature and more!

http://bookswithperks.square.site

We are also on social media!

Instagram, Facebook and TikTok account:
@bookswithperks

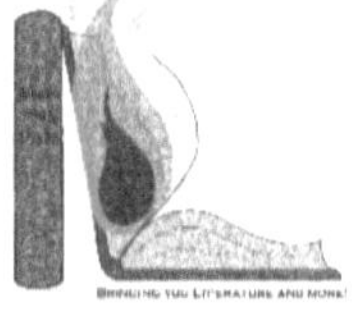

Darkness Awakens

Book 2

Red's Revenge

Part 1

Red's Origin

Three Hundred Years Later.

Chapter I

What big ears you have

I was walking in the woods dressed in a wrinkled old dress covered with a tattered shawl, back hunched over, and leaning heavily on my walking stick. At least, that's what any passerby would see. Much to Kagami's disappointment, I preferred to travel like this. Most people don't think an old lady like me is worth their time. Kagami would much prefer we appear as a beautiful young maiden, but over the years she has come to the realization that I am right every once in a while.

All I could make out past my poor vision was the long shadows stretching across the ground away from the dim light fading in the distance. Nightfall was coming soon, but that didn't matter much; I was following an aura. Not anything seen, but something felt.

I had tracked this presence across the world

these past few centuries, never getting close enough to be noticed, but always watching, waiting, learning. Because one day, I would be the one to destroy it forever.

Shirayuki, my biggest regret and oldest - human- friend. When she was just 13, she used dark magic to turn herself into a demon that had no heartbeat and survived off of only human blood. She was also impossible to kill. Trust me. I tried. It didn't go over well.

She ruled Nihon, or Japan as most of the world knows it by, for many years before her control was threatened and she decided to move on and see the world. That, or she got bored. She had traveled many places, but for the past 50 years she had resided here in Transylvania.

Her aura reeked of darkness and was easy to follow, especially after she fed. And she had been feeding a lot lately. I couldn't help but wonder if she was planning something.

That's why I was venturing far closer than I had ever dared in the past. I needed to know if the rumors were true.

As I trekked across the countryside towards Transylvania, I chatted with my constant companion. We merged after an unfortunate encounter with Shirayuki that would have killed me if we hadn't merged. Now we lived as two minds in one being: Kagami, a kitsune with a specialty in fire elemental magic, and me, Yumi, an Itako. A portion of Kagami's magic stabilized me and prevented me from aging, so while I had been alive for many hundreds of years, I looked like a 27-year-old woman. But, for now, Kagami had wrapped an illusion around us to appear as an old woman as we journeyed closer to Shirayuki's territory.

"Wow," I heard a voice of a young girl say behind me. "What are you?"

I turned towards the speaker and said, "Excuse me?" My voice came out old and frail to match my appearance.

"What are you?" she asked again.

Puzzled, I tilt my head to the side.

"I'm just an old grandma," I said.

She laughed, "Yeah, okay 'grandma'." Her voice dripped with sarcasm.

She doesn't believe us. Kagami whispered in my mind.

"You don't think an old woman like me is a grandma?" I asked.

She scoffed. "Okay, 'old woman'. What's up with your ears?"

My face burned, and it took every ounce of control to gently place my hand on the side of my head where the illusion's ears would be, not the top.

"My ears?" I ask.

"Yeah, they are so big."

"Well, all the better to hear you with." I forced a smile through gritted teeth. Hundreds of years, and I was still uncomfortable when I was reminded of my true form.

"Wow, your teeth are huge too!" she exclaimed.

"All the better to bite little girls who ask rude questions with!" My mouth moved on its own. The voice is no longer disguised as a frail old woman and is smooth as silk despite the sharp tone. Kagami had snapped in frustration and taken over my voice.

"Why did you sound different just then?"

"Why do you ask so many questions?" I countered.

"And what's with your eyes? They are all unfocused."

I blinked back my shock; this girl was blunter

than I had ever dared to be. "I'm blind."

I turned to walk away. I didn't have time to deal with a child who should be at home at this hour anyway.

But instead of letting me leave, she stepped towards me and yanked my shawl off my back.

"That is a tail!" she said triumphantly.

Rage burned through my veins as I spun around. What little light I could see turned red as Kagami took over in her anger.

"Look here, you little red hat. You need to learn to keep your questions and hands to yourself or you will find yourself in a whole lot of trouble." A rumble grew in my chest as Kagami growled, sneering at the little girl.

"And it's tails, plural, thank you very much!"

"What are you?" she whispered. I could tell from the quiver in her voice that she was on the verge of tears.

Kagami, don't scare her. I chided.

She deserves it. If it had been anyone else they would have done a lot worse, believe you me! Gawking at my beauty is one thing, but mocking? I'll show her exactly who she-

Just stop it. I cut Kagami off. *I'll handle her.*

Right, because the silver-tongued fox isn't capable of handling a little girl.

Kagami...

I turned towards the young girl and smoothed my skirts around my legs, making sure to keep our tails out of sight behind them.

"Hey, it's alright," I said in a soothing tone. "I didn't mean that, I'm sorry."

She didn't respond.

"What are you doing out so late?" I asked.

"I'm visiting my grandmother in Transylvania." she said.

"All by yourself?"

"Well yeah, I'm not a kid. I might be older than you!"

I laughed. "I highly doubt that."

"You can't be more than 12. I'm 14."

"Why would you think I'm 12?" I asked.

"Because you're so short," she said simply.

"But I'm an old grandma," I said.

"No. You're dressed like an old grandma, but you have no wrinkles and flawless skin, not to mention the..." she cleared her throat. "Other stuff."

My limbs froze as she spoke, a smile plastered on my face as I realized what she was saying.

She could see through Kagami's illusion. She saw me for me. A 27-year-old immortal girl who has merged with a spirit fox and taken on some of her traits, including canine teeth, ears, and 7 tails. Along with flawless, youthful skin.

"How can you see me?" Kagami gritted my teeth and growled.

"Well, I'm not blind!" the girl scoffed.

"Don't make fun, that's rude!" Kagami snapped.

"No, I didn't, I... what is happening?"

"I'll tell you what's going to happen if you don't start apologizing to Yumi you little - "

"We just want to know what you see when you look at us. Me," I cut off Kagami before she could start suggesting violence.

"We?" the girl asked.

"Me."

"But you said-"

"Just answer the question!" Kagami snapped again.

"Okay! I see a girl with midnight black hair and furry fox ears poking out of the top of her head. They are ink black, fading to a deep red before getting lost in your hair. You have brown eyes, sharp teeth like a wolf, or a fox would I guess. You are wearing old lady clothes, and your shawl was covering up a bushy red tail tipped in white. Or maybe tails? I didn't get a good look. What do *you* see when you look at *me*?"

The last question was obviously sarcasm, but I still had the urge to respond.

"Nothing, I'm blind." I said out of reflex. I barely got the words out when Kagami took control of my voice once again.

"You are a stringy little girl in a red hooded cloak who thinks she knows everything, and it will get her killed one day. That's what I see." Kagami huffed in anger.

"I thought you were blind."

"I am," I said.

"She is," Kagami helped.

"What is happening?" the girl asked again.

"Don't even think about it, Yumi," Kagami warned aloud to stop me from using my voice.

"My name's not..." the girl started to say.

"We can't have her spreading rumors," I reasoned.

"I can erase her memory," Kagami argued.

"We are not doing that. We don't even know if it will work! She saw right through your illusion magic."

"Details!" Kagami exclaimed. "It will be fine, a good hit to the head and she will think it all to be a dream."

"Kagami!" I warned, dropping my walking stick and clasping my hands tight behind my back so they don't betray me.

"What is going on!" The girl yelled.

"Shh!" We hissed.

I took a deep breath and closed my eyes.

She could help us, I spoke in my mind.

She is a child and she's annoying, Kagami complained.

I was her age when we met, I told her. *And really, if you didn't want her to find out, you should have stayed quiet instead of arguing with me in front of her.*

I don't know what it is about her, but she is trouble, not to mention annoying.

Stop pouting, you know you're still my favorite.

Kagami huffed, but didn't protest anymore, so I opened my eyes and said:

"What's your name?"

"Red."

To be continued...